Bone Hunter

Thea Atkinson

CHAPTER 1

I TASTED BLOOD.

As surprising as it was to have the metallic flavor tease my tongue, I didn't panic. Not at first. The taste of blood was something I got used to over the years living with Scottie. Part and parcel of the lifestyle as it were.

Like many women caught in a tangle of love and fear, I got normalized to so many things, not the least of which was the feel of a cut lip and the taste of blood. I knew the coppery tang against the insides of my cheeks as intimately as I knew the curve of my lover's thigh.

It's not something a gal easily forgets when it's an almost weekly occurrence.

Trouble was, I'd left Scottie years ago.

And I hadn't bitten my tongue.

Except for the cat sitting on the kitchen counter, swiping at the mounds of bubbles that filled the sink, I was alone in my brownstone apartment.

Alone.

I had to repeat that to myself. I was alone in a building glamored by someone from the supernatural community to keep out mortal men like Scottie and every manner of extraordinary creature that might want to do me harm.

Not the least of which was the incubus I'd blackmailed in order to attain the glamor.

It wasn't an honest acquisition of the safeguard, but it was a safeguard, and I'd never been obsessive about gaining things in an honest way.

I still wasn't quite comfortable knowing a supernatural world seethed beneath my feet, but I felt safer than I had in years when the glamor went on the brownstone.

Which was why it took me a few moments of reflection to feel afraid.

Even so, fear is a tricky thing. It does what it wants, slips into hidden mental crannies where it shouldn't. It kicks in the door whether it's reasonable or not. And despite my rationalization of knowing I was alone and hadn't been struck by a meaty fist, I had to clutch the edge of the counter to keep from bolting the way instinct screamed at me to do.

That too, came from normalizing very un-normal things.

I ran down the reasons I shouldn't be afraid again, just for good measure, and this time came up with an explanation that could explain exactly why a gal in her kitchen, doing a few dishes, could so vividly taste the tang of blood.

I'd been letting my mind wander because I hated the chore. And I'd been thinking about Scottie.

Struck with boredom and filled with a loathing for scrubbing two-day-old restaurant lasagna off the fourth plate, my mind had decided to play hooky and had slipped back to a night when I'd still loved him, and he'd lost a half a fortune to a petty thief who convinced him he was better at breaking into unique locks than any young slip of a girl could be.

Scottie hadn't trusted the guy the way he trusted me, but he was greedy. The thought that he might have an additional jimmy-jammer on his team was too much to resist, even for the careful and OCD Scottie.

He'd sent the new guy out on a heist, but the kid never came back.

I was no more to Scottie in the moment he found out he'd been had than a reminder to him that he had been duped.

Scottie hated being conned. I suppose every con man does.

The difference between a regular criminal type and Scottie was that Scottie had begun his career as muscle and built his empire on the con men he acquired through that muscle.

Thinking about it had probably set some dormant dormouse synapse in my cerebral cortex into overdrive. Like fear, memory can be a powerful thing. Vivid and visceral, even. It had a taste all its own.

I wiped the back of my soapy hand across my mouth anyway. Looked at it, certain I would see the telltale blot of red against my skin, but nothing except soapy bubbles met my eye. Several of them popped along my wrist without making a sound.

It did nothing to make me feel better because dammit, that was just plain strange. And the taste had been so clear. Was still clear.

I ran my tongue along my palate, testing. Yes. Blood. Copper and electrode-tainted zinc with a bite that was like sticking your tongue on a battery.

I wiped my hands on a towel and probed inside my cheek with my finger. No tooth broken that I could tell. No sore spot on my tongue. I leaned toward the window over the sink, trying to catch my reflection in the glass.

The kitchen light hummed overhead. It sizzled and flared and then finally went out. I was in darkness for a full heartbeat before everything came back on again with a high-pitched keening of electricity.

"What in the hell," I said out loud to the cat.

She eyed me as though she thought I was going to splash her with hot dishwater.

"It's interesting that you mention hell," said a voice from behind me.

In that one second, every sense of safety fizzled into nothing.

A hundred red lights went off inside my head. A dozen alarms. My heart hammered against my ribcage twice in rapid succession at the sound of another voice. One that shouldn't have been there. It took me too long to swing around to confront the intruder.

The cat fell into the sink with a yowl and a splash that covered my shirt with hot water. She was scrambling back out even as instinct sent my hand searching for something, anything close to hand that I could use for protection.

She streaked across the floor toward my bedroom, a wet little bolt of fur who yowled as she went, and I, soaked and terrified, spun on my heel, clutching my weapon in front of me.

I moved so quickly I swept a glass from the counter onto the floor. It shattered into a spray of crystals across the tiles. I flinched in reaction and caught my breath.

I saw nothing.

The first floor was open concept and I could see all the way through to the bay windows in the front. There wasn't anyone in plain sight.

That meant whoever it was might have sneaked up the stairs that led to the empty apartment upstairs. It had been closed off by the landlord when I moved in, but that didn't mean someone hadn't crept in and made their way silently up the treads in wait. Might even be hiding there now.

I wasn't alone. Not by a long shot.

"Shit," I muttered beneath my breath and then immediately bit down on my lip.

Maybe I could imagine a voice out of long-buried memory, but the cat couldn't. If the cat heard it, then someone was there.

The question was: Where?

I had no idea how he got in, or who he was, or even where he was, but I knew I was exposed and vulnerable. My skin prickled with the knowledge.

Standing in my kitchen, at least I had the counter to my back. My bedroom was to my left, along with any number of more deadly weapons that could take a man out without having to be in close range like a knife required.

I was little, but I wasn't stupid. At least not all the time.

I tried to crane my body to see if there was a telltale shadow on the stairs, but I wasn't at the right angle. I wasn't even in the right spot to see much without taking a noisy step on the aged floorboards.

I most decidedly did not want to move. Not one hair.

There was no way I was bolting for the front door. Not until I knew the escape route was clear.

Not until I could figure out exactly where the voice had come from. As terrifying as the thought might be, I needed another sound to orient myself to where it came from.

I felt like a coward but the wimpy girl within knew she hadn't managed to survive Scottie and a nasty sorcerer plus a fae assassin from any sort of natural bravery. Bald courage was a thief's undoing.

But it wasn't going to be my undoing.

I swallowed, tasting the blood again. I could hear my own breathing. My heart raced fast and hard enough in my ears to drown out someone else breathing.

I listened hard, trying to hear the telltale sound of someone standing on the stairs just out of sight.

I considered bolting to the bedroom. The door locked from the inside. If I had to, I could dig into my heist bag and lift out the Ruger LC9 I'd purchased after my last run in with Scottie.

Glamor was all well and good, but a gal didn't stay in her apartment 24/7. I never really knew what happened to my ex-paramour after I'd left him alone to face down Finn the nasty-ass sorcerer.

Nothing else moved. No other sound came. I stood stock still for at least four minutes without one more sound giving away a potential intruder.

I knew a thief could wait silently for at least twenty in an attempt to fool an occupant and make her believe that nothing was amiss, but even so, my fingers started to relax their grip on the knife's handle. My breath let go with a wheeze.

That was when I realized something--some sort of shadow--was smudging the sofa. A shadow that had nothing to do with the setting sun outside the window falling behind the rooftops of neighborhood houses.

A man-sized shadow that was slowly being poured out of the light spilling through the Eastern window and onto my sofa.

I watched in a kind of stupor as it solidified into a man-shaped body. His hair had a salt-and-pepper quality even if his face showed no sign of age. There was keen intelligence in that face. The eyes sparked purple for a second then settled into an icy blue.

Not human, my mind whispered.

He was splayed out against the cushions, with one arm stretched across its plaid-patterned back in a way that indicated he had been sitting there for several moments, waiting for me to notice him and was surprised I didn't.

But at least he didn't look like he was about to pounce. If he'd come to kill me, he'd have tried something by now.

My fist clenched on the knife handle as I tried to figure out what he was. Another sorcerer like Finn? Had Scottie found a way to send a supernatural minion to claim me? Had he been stalking the outside of my apartment, watching me climb invisible stairs and disappear into a solid wall all these weeks?

Whoever he was, I knew it was entirely too late to run.

CHAPTER 2

I DECIDED IN LIGHT of the way I was already standing with a knife in my hand, and him on the couch looking far too comfortable, that the best plan of attack was attack. Like a small dog facing down a bigger one, I put a lot of bark in my voice.

"What in the hell do you want?" I demanded.

At least my voice was somewhat calm. If there was a tremor in it, a hitch at the last syllable, he might mistake it for indignation instead of terror.

I wasn't about to take a chance on that though.

I stuck the knife out in front of me.

"Just what do you think you're going to do with a butter knife?" he said.

Long fingers tapped a short rhythm against the back cushion. Small puffs of dust rose to the air.

I took a careful step sideways, aiming the admittedly useless butter knife at him nonetheless. My stomach felt clammy from the wet t-shirt.

I tried to keep my voice steady. But I knew its tenor too well to know I wasn't succeeding. I just hoped he wouldn't know.

"Who are you and what do you want?"

He cocked a silver eyebrow above a gaze that shifted from blue to red and blue again.

"If you must use a name," he said. "Then you can call me Colin."

"Well, Colin," I said, edging even more toward my bedroom. "You best tell me what the hell you're doing here and how in the hell you got in."

"Who do you think put the glamor on this seedy little building?" he said.

I eyed him through narrowed lids. "I'm guessing that would be you," I said.

He placed a long finger against his nose.

"It still doesn't tell me why you're here."

"Doesn't it?" he said.

My mind went alight with possibilities. I had blackmailed a hedonistic little incubus to get that glamor, and now I wondered if maybe all that karma had come back to roost.

Maybe he had paid a rather lazy assassin to glamor the building for me, lull me into a sense of safety, then swoop in to take me out.

But that didn't seem right. The incubus Errol wouldn't be that cunning. He was more of a grope first ask for permission later sort.

I swallowed down the taste of blood and hitched the back of my hip against the counter for support. I had to think. This invader knew my house and the fact that I'd had it glamored. I imagined Errol the incubus could have sold that information, but I doubted it. I had too much on him.

I chewed the inside of my cheek thoughtfully as the man on the sofa watched me working my way through the dilemma. He even smiled a little, which did nothing to relieve my anxiety.

It was about then that the cat pushed her way through the crack in my bedroom doorway, dragging along her disgusting little flannel receiving blanket. The smell of wet fur hung in the air as she headed past me and jumped up into the intruder's lap.

At sight of it, my grip on the handle of the knife relaxed somewhat. She obviously was perfectly okay with him. And while she rarely made an effort to be liked by anyone, she was already arching her back against his fingers, commanding in her arrogant way to be idolized.

So much for worrying I was about to be murdered. My cat was not the petting type.

I felt my shoulders sag, but I didn't let go of my grip on the knife. Not yet.

I looked him over, trying to work out exactly what sort of creature he was. He looked far too human to be something like a Golem, too damn handsome to be a troll. Not that I would know them if I saw them. I was still new to the world of otherworldly creatures.

But I reasoned that if he had regular sized canines he couldn't be a vampire either. There might have been a sharp elongation to his jaw, but I had no idea what that meant. The best I could describe him was that he was shimmery.

Shimmery and handsome. Like flat-out beautiful.

And it was there that my knowledge of all things supernatural ended. My interest moved to more important things. Like what the hell he was doing in my apartment, trespassing the heck out of it, in fact.

"You might have glamored my house, but it doesn't give you the right to door-crash it."

"I didn't..." he started to say, then shrugged with such elegance that I might have liked him. "I don't know what door-crashing is," he admitted.

I clenched my fists next to my side, undeterred. "It means you've entered where you have no rights. This is my home. Mine."

He grinned, showing me a set of teeth that glittered like crystal.

"Technically, it's *my* home," he said. He buried his face in the cat's fur and she purred loud enough to make me glare at her.

"Come again?" I said.

"Glamor isn't really a specialty," he explained. "It's a cheap trick and nothing more. The problem with something being glamored is that it still exists exactly as it is."

He shrugged casually at the words but there was nothing unassuming about it. It was a deliberate affectation, as though he was working hard at seeming human.

"Errol asked me for glamor. I gave you glamor," he continued. "For about three days. Then I gave you something more lasting." He paused for a moment. "Something safer."

He stressed the last word.

"Doesn't seem so safe to me," I said, jerking my chin at him to indicate how safe I thought it was if he could just stroll in.

He ignored the implication.

"Should someone stumble upon your little apartment door in your world, the magic might not have been enough to keep them fooled. I had to do something far more permanent. For your safety, you understand."

"My safety," I repeated. The skin on the back of my neck prickled.

He inclined his head ever so slightly. I thought I could smell warm toffee.

"No doubt this safety comes at a cost," I said.

He rubbed the cat's ears until she leaned against him, greedy for the touch.

"Doesn't everything?" he said and stretched out his legs as the cat rolled over, trying to lay enough scent on him to claim him as hers.

I cursed out loud and resisted the urge to scoop her from his lap.

"So if my building isn't glamored," I said, "then what is it? Some sort of spell?"

His brow wrinkled, and I guessed I'd agitated him with the word spell.

"It's very specific magic," he said with a tightness to his voice that told me I was right. "The house itself is still settled nicely in the ninth world. But the interior you are in--that we are in--exists in my realm. The Fourth world. Much older than yours."

He flashed that crystal grin again. "Should someone else come into your building in the mortal realm, they will see what you expect. A dank stairway. A disgustingly cluttered apartment. Lots of socks and shoes strewn about."

At that, he peered about the room with a look of careful politeness and my eye fell on a pair of socks I'd pulled off and left at the foot of the sofa.

I shifted as I stood there, remembering that those socks had been stuffed in hot boots the day before as I'd staked out a museum curator's extracurricular storage locker for several sweltering hours.

"Okay," I said feeling the prickle of embarrassment. "So you've been to my real apartment. Big deal. If I'm not there, then where am I?"

"I told you. The fourth world. When you enter your dank little--"

I held up a hand. "Enough with the dank, already," I said, feeling irritated now instead of afraid.

I dropped the knife onto the counter with a clatter. If he hadn't hurt me by now, he had no intentions of it and I was tiring of the guessing game. I wanted answers.

"So?" I demanded.

He smiled. "You enter your building like anyone else does, but for you the threshold is different. When you cross it, you enter the duplicate I made for you in my world."

"And where does this threshold cross, exactly?"

He grinned, looking pleased with himself. "My manor."

I blinked stupidly. There were far too many awful things in that information for me to decide on just one question to ask. I had to settle for one, and my brain latched onto the word threshold.

"So the threshold is a portal of some sort?"

I couldn't keep the tremor from my voice as I thought of the Blood Gate at the Shadow Bazaar. The bazaar itself was every bit as shadowy as its name and I'd not seen even a quarter of it when I'd been there.

It had been long over a month since I'd been sent in to meet its owner by one of my networking homeless teens. That owner turned out to have connections to the pawn shops I frequented to unload my less valuable items.

Maddox. The name came to me as it had many times over the weeks, with an effortless glide. And yet, I shivered involuntarily, and not from a vestige of peculiar desire my body wanted to remind me of for the man and his peculiar charisma, but because the portal into his bazaar was nasty.

I couldn't help thinking or wondering what might be happening to me unaware every time I crossed into my building from the street.

I crossed my arms over my chest without meaning to.

"I've experienced one of your portals before," I said. "The Blood Gate."

"I've heard of it, but it's not one of mine, I must admit," he said. "Nor is it of fae. Our magic is more powerful than that. The Blood Gate is nothing but crude enchantment meant to dissuade unsavouries."

"Unsavouries meaning humans," I guessed.

He rubbed the cat's belly and she flopped over, legs in the air. She never did that for me. I stomped over to push her onto the floor. She gave me a baleful stare before walking stiff-legged to her water bowl.

The intruder leaned forward, hanging his hands between his knees as he peered up at me. I tapped my foot, but it was all for show. I knew it was nervous energy. I just hoped he wouldn't figure that out.

I stuffed my hands in my pockets so he wouldn't see them shake. What was I doing baiting a creature I knew nothing about except that he held the keys to keeping my brownstone safe from Scottie's eyes?

"Regardless," I said. "I'm not so sure I like the thought of you popping into my house any time you want."

His eyebrows lifted. "Did I pop? I would think I'd make a more dignified entrance."

"You know what I mean."

He smiled again and this time I caught the distinct glint of gold. I tried to look without staring, but I could swear it wasn't gold capping. I didn't realize he'd spoken until he nudged my toe with his foot.

"What did you say?" I asked, my vision clearing.

"I said maybe we could make a deal."

"I don't make deals with people I don't know."

He chuckled. "Forgive me," he said. "I didn't exactly make myself clear. I need you to do something for me."

I had the feeling what he planned to ask was going to be very unpleasant.

"And if I don't?"

He smiled again. But this time, the glint of gold disappeared and there was the distinct look of clotted blood clinging to his teeth, pooled behind the corners of his grin.

I got an incredibly vivid flash of him washing blood from armor while women all around him wailed inconsolably.

He cocked his head sideways.

"I'd tell you, but I don't want to scare you."

CHAPTER 3

I TOOK AN INVOLUNTARY step backward as he rose from the sofa. He wasn't tall, not in the conventional sense. I was what a kind teacher had once called diminutive and while almost everyone seemed big to me, he didn't loom over me like most people did.

Even so, there was something about the way he moved, the way he stood that made him seem large. Like he expected everyone to react as though he was seven feet tall.

I had the feeling that everyone did exactly that.

He moved like a fighter, graceful and intentional, keeping his arms tight against his body. Scottie moved like that and I'd know a scrapper anywhere.

And yes. He was intentionally trying to intimidate me. We both knew it. Worse, it was working, and he could see the effect on me. I had only to look into his eyes to know that.

I moved away from him instinctively, leaning away, keeping my arms tight against my body. I had to crane my neck to see up into his face because I wasn't about to lose sight of those eyes with him so close.

If I'd learned anything from Scottie it was that violence flashed through the eyes before it flashed through a fist. I didn't think my visitor would use anything so crude as a punch to subdue me, but if he planned on anything else, I might be able to make a break for it.

Or at least brace myself for impact.

I followed him with my gaze as he made a wide berth around me to stroll toward the counter where shards of broken glass still glinted against the tiled floors as they caught the light.

The chemical scent of lilac drifted to me in his wake. The dish detergent, not him. He smelled even stronger of toffee. And something else I couldn't name.

He stared down at the floor for several seconds before he spun on his heel, more gracefully than a man should be able to, and faced me.

"Do you wonder if a glass falls here in your wing of my manor, if it also falls and breaks in your human world?"

It was a strange question and I stuttered out a response that made me wonder what the heck I was even on about. I chalked my pleasant sense of ineloquence up to a bolt of nervous energy.

I wasn't surprised when he gave a mute shake of his head at my inarticulate response, but I was surprised when he reached for the broom that lay against the outside door of the broom closet--exactly where I'd left it the week before when I'd swept up spilled dry cat food so the cat wouldn't scarf it down in one sitting and puke it up on my bed later.

I watched him sweep the tiles with elegant but waspish strokes. He sent me a disapproving glare once or twice as he dug at crystals in the grout and came away with a good bit of potato chip crumbs as well. I thought I caught sight of a crust of toast.

I crossed my arms. My house. If he didn't like the state of it, he could leave. I said so, in fact.

He grunted beneath his breath but said nothing. I guessed he didn't like it, but that he wasn't about to leave.

He lifted the biggest chunk, the thick bottom with jagged, sharp edges, and set it on its base on the counter beside the trash.

When he had the rest of the glass shards arranged into a neat pile on the floor, he lifted his eyebrow at me.

I pointed silently at the closet and he opened the door to extract the dustpan. He spoke again only when he had scooped up the last of the glass and deposited it into the trash bin.

"So?" he said. "Have you?"

He brushed at his trousers and looked down at his fingers, rubbing them together with delicate fastidiousness.

"Have I what?" I said, mesmerized by the movement of his fingers.

I thought I saw a shimmer of color wavering around his skin as he nudged the broken glass bottom toward the middle of the counter. It winked with blue light like a sale strobe in a cheap department store.

"Have you thought about what happens to the glass in your real apartment?" he said again.

I lifted one shoulder deferentially. "Never had reason to wonder," I told him.

He put the broom away. "Fair enough," he said. "But it's a good question all the same. What do you think?"

I shook my head. I wasn't sure what the answer should be or even if it was safe to guess. There were all sorts of reasons I wanted the glamor I'd blackmailed Errol for.

Looking at my visitor--I couldn't call him an intruder anymore since apparently I was in his home and not my own--and taking in the way he was imperiously awaiting my answer, I added one more to the list.

It occurred to me that visitor or intruder shouldn't matter; surely, I had still some rights.

"Maybe I should ask you the questions," I said carefully. "Like why you're here. And how you got in."

My bluntness surprised even me, and I clamped my mouth closed with a click of my teeth.

He chuckled amiably but without a shred of authenticity.

"Your cat is a far friendlier creature than you are," he said.

I managed to shrug and hoped it looked casual because the way my shoulder felt, all tense and frozen, I had the feeling it looked more like a jerky marionette limb.

"Cats are weird things anyway," I said. "Mine even more so."

"You don't have a name for her?" he asked.

I shrugged. I hadn't needed one. Cat worked just fine.

He sighed. "I could always put you back in your own apartment to see if there's a broken glass on the floor," he said, getting back to the point. "Maybe it's cleaned up and in the trash bin like this one is."

He jerked his chin toward the garbage. "Or maybe there is no other apartment anymore. Maybe you're already 'home'."

He leaned against the counter with his arms crossed and one foot over the other. "I wonder what you'd think then."

He didn't look very murderous, the way he stood there leaning against my counter, his ankles crossed, but the undercurrent of his tone was most definitely so, and the words were about as threatening as anything I'd heard from Scottie.

Experience taught me that some men could be the most terrifying when he acted the most casual.

"You're threatening me," I said.

Whatever veil of civility my visitor was stretching over his patience was beginning to wear. He sighed and planted his palms on the counter, drummed his fingertips against the sideboard. "You're a difficult one," he said. "A strange little human."

I stuffed my hands in my jeans pockets. It wasn't the first time I'd heard it in the last few weeks. No matter how anxious I was, I was determined not to show it.

"You don't want to guess?" he said. "About the glass?"

This time his tone wasn't merely questioning the way a stranger might ask you your occupation. This time it was a command.

I picked what seemed the most important considering the dread that crept up my spine.

"I have a feeling there's something in my true apartment that I'd like seeing less than what might have happened to a cheap dime store glass."

I knew the truth only when I said it out loud. He didn't need to tell me.

"What is it?" I said.

"Wouldn't you rather know the very simple thing you can do to avoid finding out?"

My stomach felt as though someone had dropped a blob of cement down my gullet. I had the awful feeling I knew exactly why he was there.

Shades of Finn and the awful, horrible, near-death task of finding a rune tile flashed through my memory. Coupled with my earlier mental image of this visitor washing blood off armour into a pool at his feet, and I lost all my bravado.

I ran my hand along the back of my neck as though someone had slid a garrote over it while I wasn't looking.

The cat jumped up on the counter, pulling along her blankie along with her like a rat's tail, and shoving it against his hand. She was still growing out the hair that Finn had singed down to her skin and had taken to using the blanket for warmth when she wasn't hogging my pillow at night.

My visitor wadded it up and made a nest of it that he set in the empty side of the sink. She burrowed in and rattled out a loud purring sound.

I glared at her, the little traitor, but I aimed my words at him, thinking I could logic my way out of whatever he wanted.

"What makes you think I'm the person who should do this thing, whatever it is?"

"I don't think it, I know it. Of course, a woman such as yourself understands the value of a transaction."

I straightened up, reading that to mean I would get something in return for whatever he wanted of me, and I didn't have to think too long to know what that was.

"You'll leave the magic on the building if I agree," I said.

He nodded.

"And if I don't?"

He canted his head to the side and for a moment looked very boyish.

"I know a lot about you, Ms. Hush," he said. "One might say I'm the kind of fae who shouldn't know too much about a mortal woman."

Fae. Like the assassin who had trailed me and tried to kill me for Finn's rune tile. The back of my neck went clammy.

"You're threatening me again." I wanted to sound confident, but it came out as a squeak. So much for my bravado.

He smiled. "Threats are for weaker creatures than me. I'm simply stating a fact."

He lifted his index finger in the air. "Fact one: you owe me. And I have all the--what do you call it--intel?" he said.

He wouldn't look me in the eye when he said intel. That couldn't be good.

He lited the next finger and the next. "Fact two: you have enemies. Fact three: you would like to remain invisible from said enemies."

He'd hit on every single thing, of course, that mattered to me at the moment. I'd stayed in the city because of the anonymity when I could have hit the bricks.

The glamor had allowed me to stay where I'd cultivated a good network of intelligence and contacts. Contacts that were paid were not friends. They had no stake in my safety. Except for a bartender and a skinny teen who provided me word on potential grifts or heists, I had no one.

So, yes, each of those things was true. But not because there was no choice in any of them.

I reached into the dry side of the double sink and pulled out the purring cat. She had the nerve to hiss at me and I tossed her toward the bedroom, letting the blankie sail along behind her before I faced him again.

"Fact four," I argued. "I don't need to stay here. I can live elsewhere, equally invisible from these enemies."

I put air quotes around the last and he chuckled before hitching himself most indelicately up to the countertop.

He swung his legs in a boyish way. "Would you care to hear facts five and six?"

I didn't answer, but he gave them anyway.

"Fact five: You've been following a lead on a new archaeological discovery that just so happens to be an affair I've been following as well for my own personal interest. Fact six, and perhaps seven as well: Your lover is still alive, and he is still much interested in knowing exactly where it is you've got to."

CHAPTER 4

A fae knew enough about me to know I would be terrified to discover my lover was alive. For some reason, Maddox's face came to mind with his strangely attractive squashed nose and burnished hair. I brushed thought of him away impatiently. I'd had enough of dangerous men and he'd indicated he thought I was nothing but a foolish human.

No. I knew who my visitor meant by lover. A man I'd left for dead with Finn. The man I'd run from, the man who had ordered one of his thugs to teach me a lesson.

"Scottie is alive?" I said.

The last I'd seen of Scottie he was facing down that angry sorcerer completely oblivious to his own threat of demise. I'd seen that he'd somehow come into possession of one of the Odin runes Finn had me fetch, and if anything, the sorcerer would claim that property with much violence and little empathy.

If this fae creature said Scottie was alive, I had no doubt he was.

"So what is this task, then?" I said, testing the waters.

The fae man grinned widely. The teeth that showed shifted back to gold and crystal. His eyes went the most delirious shade of blue.

"I need you to retrieve something that was stolen."

"Sounds like a job for a supernatural police force, not a thief hiding behind fae glamor."

"You're assuming there is such a thing."

I sighed, not liking where this was going. "Then why not just fetch it yourself?"

He pursed his lips. "A sidhe warlord does not fetch."

He didn't put air quotes around the word fetch, but his tone implied it. I had no idea what sidhe was, but I wasn't fool enough to let the label of warlord pass me by.

I ran my hand through my hair and scratched at my scalp.

"So what is this thing you want me to retrieve? And what will I get out of it?"

I was pleased at finding a suitable replacement for the offensive fetch.

"The body and bones of a god."

I quirked a brow despite myself. "Bones of a god?" I sucked the back of my teeth. "Finding out who stole them is a tall enough order on its own, but getting them back?" I wavered my hand back and forth. "Sounds like a job for someone who cares."

"Oh I know who stole them."

"You do?"

"Oh yes." His legs stopped swinging as he regarded me with all seriousness. "Vampires."

His words made the skin on my back crawl.

I immediately recalled the vampire I had encountered in the Shadow Bazaar, a place like nothing I'd ever seen before and hoped never to go to again. Indeed, the only way I'd got in the first time had been through some spell or something that my strange young contact, Kassie, wove for me. I hadn't given it much thought at the time, since I'd been in a perpetual state of panic, but if she could weave a spell to get me into the bazaar, she had to be some sort of witch.

If I could find the prodigal girl, I might be able to have some help with this new task should I choose to take it on.

Because I'd need help if vampires were involved.

That vampire from the bazaar was nothing like the sexy vamps of *True Blood* or *Dark Shadows*, or even *The Vampire Diaries*. I could love me some Damon even if he wanted to drain me down to the last pint...but that vampire from the bazaar?

My skin crawled at thought of him like it wanted to dance on its own without bones or muscles to hold it upright.

"You said vampires," I said just to be sure.

"Yes," the warlord said.

His legs were making me dizzy and I reached out to stop them swinging.

"Not the sparkly Edward Cullen kind or the sexy Damon or Eric kind," I said. I had to ask again. Just to be clear. "Real Bela Lugosi vamps. The kind that drink human blood."

He pursed his lips thoughtfully. "All blood actually," he said. "They prefer human blood but aren't too picky in a pinch."

He was being entirely too amiable with this information. It couldn't possibly bode well.

I thought of Fayed, my bartender friend at the Rot Gut Tavern. I was pretty sure after my last visit that he was a vampire and he was pretty damn sexy even for a mortal man. So maybe they didn't all have to be dangerous and deadly revolting like the ones in the Bazaar.

"So these vampires," I said. "Why can't you send one of your fae minions to do this thing?"

He smiled. "Didn't you watch *True Blood*?" he said.

I hitched in a breath without meaning to. Had he just read my mind?

"Why do you ask?" I said, wary.

"Most fae won't get in the way of a vampire. We taste too good."

"Why do I think you're pulling my leg?"

He shrugged. "Maybe I am. Or maybe I just want you to repay a little kindness with kindness. Maybe you just owe me, and I want my due."

This last was said with a sort of baldness to it, like he wanted me to pay attention to the words.

I chewed the inside of my cheek.

I had the feeling it wasn't because he couldn't retrieve the relic himself or that he was too important to fetch it. He was keeping from me his motivation and was exploiting my position for his own gain.

Not that it bothered me. I'd been exploited plenty during my lifetime for far less than the ideal of safety.

The real problem was that except for Fayed and the vampires in the bazaar, I had no network or connections to the vampire world. I hadn't heard from Kassie since I'd lost her when I'd jumped the portal to the bazaar back into my own world.

And I *did* have that other lead. One I'd already invested a lot of time in. I'd watched word of the excavation for weeks via a back channel to a social media group set up to show the fascinating items pulled one by one from the muck of a peat bog in Wales.

Fragments of pots, spoons, torques, and a tantalizing glimpse of a bog mummy believed to be the legendary brother of Chu Chulain who had killed his brother in a jealous rage. The cache was said to rival Tut's tomb, and our humble museum had it all.

But the most interesting things were the hushed and coded mentions of things they couldn't show. The entire cache was rumored to be hastily cataloged with dozens of artifacts still uncatalogued or cataloged under time duress, a most unusual thing for a museum acquisition.

Filled with tiny trinkets and larger items alike, the dig had been fraught with firings and theft from start to finish.

A perfect opportunity for the light fingered and criminal minded.

And it was all going to be on display, right down to the bogman and all those pottery shards and jewelry, along with numerous smaller items, including a coin of some sort covered in electrum and stamped with a symbol that language specialists were still arguing over.

It was delicious, the thought of all those undocumented items, small and large just waiting in a storage basement for someone to appreciate them on deep, economic and mercenary level.

One thing the fae warlord had not mentioned was the patronage exhibit was in about four hours. All those heavy financial hitters and their plus ones would get first peek at the goods before the rest of the world, and hopefully foot more money to continue the search for 'items undoubtedly still lying invitro to be rescued from Mother Earth's womb.

I'd already picked out my gown and heels and found a sleek ginger colored wig that would just touch my shoulders. The dress had no back and very little front, and most guards I knew ogled cleavage no matter how much they were paid to be diligent.

I was as good as in.

But it wasn't the wig and dress that was the showstopper. It was my very own QR code ticket, altered to bring up the website of a surveillance video from a camera I'd installed a week earlier.

For a man who made a living with old things, I happened to know the curator had a fancy for all things young and he owed a good deal of money to a high classed escort agency that specialized in acquisitions for those who had 'alternate' tastes.

I had a revolting forty seconds of video on a masked cloud drive with a time limit to destruction. A one time viewing opportunity and I couldn't let it go to waste.

Of course, the curator wouldn't know that. I planned to trade that forty seconds for ten minutes alone with the un-catalogued items while the gala unfurled in all its glory. I had stashed a heist bag in the dumpster out back big enough to hold a few smaller items that no one would miss.

A fair trade, in my humble opinion, compared to a job for a fae I really didn't need.

The surveillance set up had cost me dearly from my bug-out stash and I was far too close to abandon now to go on a goose chase of fae proportions.

"Not a goose chase," the fae warlord said, indicating I'd said some of that out loud. Or worse, that he was reading my mind. He swirled his toe in the air, studying it with a little too much attention I thought.

"My task for you is real. And it's life or death for you."

Whether the vampires were sparkly or not, I wasn't ready to get mixed up in the supernatural 'other world' again. It had cost me too much even if it had provided me pretty good cover for the last month. But if someone, namely this someone, had the key to my front door, what good was the lock?

Besides, my accidental foray into this other world had cost me a perfectly good networking connection.

Poor Kassie was no doubt still in hiding after her experience with it. I'd thought about her a dozen times a week, telling myself she'd pop up when she was ready. She had yet to show, proof that she was beyond traumatized.

And there was something about the way he looked at his foot, to be honest, that bothered me. I crossed my arms over my chest as I regarded him.

I shook my head, deciding finally.

"Doesn't matter," I said. "I'm not going to do it. If the gala pans out, I can move if I have to. No worries about Scottie."

He eased down from the counter and canted his head at me. If he was surprised I would refuse, he showed only a mild disappointment. It was the way his eyes sparked purple and then fire red before they settled back into the icy blue that revealed the most.

Maybe some normal folks mistook that beautiful blue for a calm and restful sky. I knew the calm before the storm always looked peaceful like that.

I guessed he wasn't used to being refused.

I tapped my fingers against my biceps.

"It's not a good time," I said, trying to drive home the refusal while at the same time softening the blow. I might not want to fetch some bones for him, but I didn't want him zapping me into Kingdom Come either.

"I was willing to ask," he said slowly, enunciating each syllable clearly. "In light of you being new to the world of the fae, I thought to try the mortal way. But I am warning you. If you owe the fae, they like to be repaid."

"But I didn't ask you for the favor," I said. Surely a race who liked to be repaid favors would understand exactly who owed them.

"True," he said. "It was Errol who requested it. But it was for you and that's a close enough affinity for me to make this small ask of you. You are benefiting from it, after all."

"Way I see it," I countered. "I paid Errol. I'm still paying Errol everyday I don't turn him in to the police. Go see him to fetch your fairy goddess bones."

His reaction to the word fairy made me think of a few less politically correct terms thrown about in the human world by some pretty bigoted folks I knew, and I realized I'd made a mistake. I might have wanted it to come out like a flippant quip but once a word like that is out it can't be retracted.

That was when he stopped acting amiable.

CHAPTER 5

I KNEW ENOUGH ABOUT the fae to know that a hostile one was as dangerous as a Mac truck about to collide into a pedestrian. I desperately did not want to be the one crossing the street—or this fae. I felt my feet shuffle backwards to the fridge.

"I was going to tell you more," he said icily. "I was going to offer everything I had to help you. Not now. Now you will have to find it all out the hard way."

He hadn't made a single move toward me, but I felt as though he was pressing me back, cornering me. My lungs squeezed out their breath in a wheeze that made my throat hurt.

He inclined his head ever so slightly toward me and I felt a rush of power emanating from him that might have moved my hair. I reached up to touch it and discovered it was still plastered against my head.

I tasted blood again. Stronger this time. My hand flew to my mouth.

"That's you, isn't it?" I whispered, knowing as soon as my fingers came away clean that the taste was something he was doing to me, that he was the reason blood had filled my mouth in the first place. Not memories of Scottie. Not biting my tongue.

Him.

He didn't answer; instead he asked me another question, one as strange as whether a glass in my real apartment broke at the same time as the fae one did.

"Do you like things easy or hard?" he said.

"What?" I said, running my fingers across my mouth to be sure the blood wasn't there.

"Easy like the button at the office supply store," he said. "But you're not the easy type, it seems."

He went all gray and blurry, the same smudgey sort of blur he'd arrived as, and I started to panic. He'd be gone and not have answered my question at all, and it seemed important.

"The taste of blood in my mouth," I said again, afraid he'd disappear completely before I could get my answer. "Tell me; is that you?"

"Did that happen?" he said as though he hadn't expected it. "You really are a strange human."

And then the smudge merely evaporated as it walked back toward the sofa, and I was left alone.

My knees felt like over-steeped teabags and I sank to the floor, my knees up to my chin.

I had the sure feeling I'd dodged a bullet, and I wasn't entirely certain I was all the way out of its path.

I sat there until the cat peeked out from the bedroom and, assuming I was on the floor to feed her, strolled out to curl in and out of the spaces between my legs.

She mewled at me once or twice before I found the energy to roll onto all fours. I crawled over to the broom closet to lift out a bag of dry food and dumped it into her bowl.

She bumped into my hand and the kibble sprayed across the floor.

I took one look at the spray of kibble and noted it had fallen into what looked like a pair of wings, taunting me.

I ran my hand through it and fisted a handful. Pebbles of it crunched in my fist.

"I've never been easy," I said to the air, and I thought I heard a dry chuckle coming from someplace I couldn't pinpoint.

The cat purred as she ate, and she stared at me over her bowl as though I planned to steal it.

"Don't worry," I told her. "I'm not destitute enough yet to eat cat food."

I pushed myself to my feet and pulled down my t-shirt. I was a big girl. Things needed to be done. No sense waiting around and feeling sorry for myself.

I had an exhibit to catch. And now that I'd ticked off what I assumed was a very powerful fae, I'd best be on that exhibit like stink on herring.

I dressed as hurriedly as I could, taking the greatest care with my makeup and wig. I'd learned the art of contouring from a foster sister back before I'd cared enough to use makeup on myself and spent endless hours in front of a mirror as her model while she practiced changing my face shape.

You don't spend that much time watching careful application and not pick up a few things. I knew I had a heart shaped face and I knew how to draw it out to give the illusion of it being longer. Fake eyelashes, a wad of highlight and contour, enough to make me feel like I was wearing a mask, gave my cheeks a sharp edge and my chin a longish angle.

More than a modicum of smoky detail to the eyelids allowed me to stretch my wide-eyed innocent look into a sultry, almost Asian affect. I stuck a beauty spot to my cheek on the left side so that if I had to be identified, they'd pick out that detail along with the hair color.

I applied a very expensive temporary tattoo in the shape of a long-stemmed black rose right in the crevice of my cleavage so that the stem dipped toward my navel and the bloom circled the curve of my left breast, which itself was much plumped up by a sticky push up cup.

I slipped in some expensive colored contacts Scottie had bought me back in the day and *voila*. Brown eyed Sue became green-eyed Ginger.

If I wanted to be anonymous, I was going about it all wrong.

But I didn't want anonymity.

I wanted something akin to it, the next best thing, actually. One thing I knew from experience was that people's memories get foggy. Even three people seeing the exact same thing will have different memories of it, depending on where they focus.

Perspective is everything.

And I was counting on putting that focus where I wanted it.

Since melting into the crowd would be impossible, I needed to exploit that small idiosyncrasy of the brain. As Isabella, I was plain and ordinary, but even plain and ordinary could get noticed under the right circumstances. A luscious redhead with a dozen other qualities for folks to focus on except her face was a sure-fire way to distract and exploit people's memories.

I wanted people to see and take note of all the wrong things.

Of course, the cat hissed at me when I exited the bedroom and into the kitchen in my six-inch stilettos that went along with the slinky khaki colored dress. Most days, I would have scooped her up and petted her to calm her fears of stranger danger.

This time, I stuck my tongue out at her and shooed her into the bedroom. I hadn't forgiven her just yet for her suck up to the fae warlord.

As was my typical practice, I left the brownstone and walked four blocks before hailing an uber from my app.

"This is fine," I told the driver when I saw the line up of impressive cars and queue of cabs. Valets were flipping keys and cabbies were spilling out three high class attendees at a time. I doubted anyone would notice one redhead in the mill of expensive RSVPs all dressed to the nines.

I strolled to the queue confidently, pulled out my QR code 'invite' that should have sent the scanner to a barcode that would immediately blip me on the way it did for each person ahead of me.

I was running my thumb along the back of it, trying to pick out the target of blackmail when I caught sight of an all-too familiar sandy head.

Scottie.

And he wasn't alone.

He had muscle with him.

A young lady that looked to be about fourteen at the maximum stood nearby, running her gaze along Scottie and his men with a certain kind of agitation.

I wasn't surprised to see Scottie hale and healthy because the fae had told me as much. But I felt crushed to see him here, all the same, right when I had an important job on my agenda.

The invite got all but crumpled in my clenched fist as I reacted despite my brain's fervent message to remain calm. He hadn't seen me yet. He might never see me. Not the real me, anyway.

I started second guessing my disguise. I'd made a mistake. Scottie loved women. He wouldn't look twice at a mousey and unassuming woman but would find a way to introduce himself to a tall, barely dressed red-head. I could at least be grateful I'd worn khaki and not a more eye-catching black or red.

I jerked my gaze toward my ex and then over to the teenaged girl. Her eyes flitted about anxiously. They never rested on a single thing long enough for me to worry about catching her eye and Scottie, following her gaze, to find me.

But I felt my gorge rise at the way he crowded her as though she wasn't there at all, the way she quailed away from him when he got too close.

It was that movement that told me all I needed to know: he was bullying her. He wanted her here and she wanted nothing to do with him.

My heart ached for the poor thing.

Scottie collected women of all ages the way a man collected antique coins or luxury cars. He didn't always take one out for a spin, but he knew they could be valuable if he held onto her long enough.

As abhorrent as the thought of what he might be doing with that young girl, I was even more afraid of what he'd do if he caught sight of me. I knew I needed to melt into the crowd, and like, yesterday.

I fumbled to pass the doorman my ticket when I felt a whisper of touch move along my bare arm.

I spun around, terrified for a moment that Scottie had actually caught sight of me and sent an unseen thug to collect me.

I came face to face with a set of eyes I'd not seen in weeks. He'd lost the man bun and his fox-colored hair was slicked back neatly behind his ears instead of his usual man-bun, but it was Maddox all the same.

His suit was another Desmond Merrion, this time a burnished sort of grey.

He looked incredible and terrifying in the same instant, because he was reason number two that my new heist was in jeopardy.

"Hello, Kitten," he said.

Maddox. My poor heart did a ridiculous flip flop at the sound of his voice. I'd met him in an alley after a bust heist, and I'd been full of blood and pepper spray. He turned out later to be the same cocky SOB in the pawn shop where I'd tried to divest myself of the wares from said botched heist.

Later still, I discovered him to be the proprietor of the Shadow Bazaar. Gorgeous, arrogant, tall Maddox.

I had to remind myself that this man dealt with supernaturals of all sorts, and by his own admission was not human. That should be enough for me to focus on the real reason I was here.

Even so, standing in the cool breeze of the museum's circular drive, poised to get inside, for a fleeting moment, my sense of vanity stroked the ego that had me wearing a sexy dress and high heels.

And then I realized one very important thing.

He should not have been able to recognize me either.

CHAPTER 6

I yanked my invite back from the doorman and wilted away from the queue uncertainly, not sure if I should melt back toward the street or keep forging ahead to the lobby. If Maddox could see through the disguise, then surely Scottie would.

I needed to haul ass out of there before I ended up pitched into a peat bog myself, somewhere discreet.

Maddox made to say something more and I swung away, pulling the string of my beaded purse along with me through a throng of genteel seniors holding colorful pamphlets. I wished for a second I hadn't worn heels at all.

The diminutive Isabella would have been able to disappear easily while the tall redheaded Ginger had to clomp along slowly and painfully, each step in fear of discovery.

Maddox followed me as I melted away from the lineup and despite me forcing as brisk a pace as I could, abruptly pushing through some rather stately divas who really shouldn't have been out so late, he kept up with me.

I felt his fingers brush against my arm.

I fumbled with my purse because I simply didn't dare look full into that green-eyed gaze, even through the windows of my colored contacts.

He edged nearer to me and had to lean so close when a patron pushed past that I felt his breath on my cheek. My heart sped up and something within made me search out Scottie's face through the crowd, afraid he'd see me with another man.

Maddox's fingers kissed the edge of my elbow, forcing my attention back to him.

"Hey," he said.

"Do I know you?" I said, trying to put the ice of a stranger's voice in the query. An inexplicable nervousness sang along the edges of my nerves.

"Ouch," he said. "I think I just heard my heart crack."

The timbre of his voice made me think of velvet and chocolate, and I flicked my gaze back to his, drawn by something I couldn't resist. I should just brush him off and keep going. I'd waited too long already to disappear.

Maybe he'd move on, thinking he'd made a mistake. I shook my head at him, deciding silence was my best option. He wasn't to be dissuaded so easily.

"You're not leaving so soon, surely," he said. "You'll miss the show."

"I changed my mind," I said, flustered. "Not that it matters to a stranger."

He canted his head to the side. "I'm not in the habit of calling strange women *Kitten*," he said.

I shivered as I caught the faintest hint of soap and smoke. My memory cast about for an image of him that was clear and perfect. I ended up snagged on the most pleasant one I had: of he and I in his office, filled with books and the finest scotch.

I remembered the little box he'd stored the rune in and the way he'd pulled a mace from the wall, ready to do battle with the fae assassin who had door-crashed his bazaar.

I shuffled sideways at the memory, my heels nearly buckling and reminding me I was in a dress and rather uncomfortable shoes.

One side of his mouth tugged up as he watched me fidgeting, and I found I had a hard time pulling my eyes from the small dimple just at the fleshiest part of his cheek.

"In fact," he said. "I call only one woman by that nickname." He snicked in tight enough to my side that his lips brushed my earlobe. "But she's not a redhead and certainly isn't as tall as you."

At that moment, someone pushed into us and he caught me with one broad hand on the small of my back as I jostled sideways. It was a reflexive movement, I knew, one a gentleman did without thinking when someone next to him nearly tumbles, but something in the way his fingers splayed across the curve of my hip made me flush.

I stammered out something about needing to get inside and he scooped my chin with his fingers so I had to look him in the eye where he could search my face.

Damn those eyes. They could melt the panties off a blow-up doll. I swallowed down the clump that tightened my throat when his gaze dropped to my mouth and then down to the stem of the rose tattoo. I hoped it looked real under that careful scrutiny, one that made no apologies for lingering so long.

"I owe you an apology then," he said. "A case of mistaken identity, we'll call it." The dimple appeared again.

I knew he was teasing me and I should have given up the pretense, but just when I thought I should, a willowy blonde with hair so light it looked like spun silver sauntered over, waving what looked like liquor tickets over her head.

All thoughts of revealing myself sailed down the gutter along with one of the tickets that escaped her manicured fingers.

She sidled up next to him, slipping an arm into his elbow and molding her entire body into his side. She didn't so much as give me a glance. I supposed she didn't think there was any competition worth looking over.

"I scored five extra champagne slips," she purred and actually licked his earlobe.

I was annoyed to see she didn't have to strain upward to do so, even though Maddox was a good six foot four. I told myself I would not look at her shoes. Mine were high enough and I only reached his Adam's apple. If hers were flat, I was going to choke on my annoyance.

His eyes left mine and slid over his date as he extracted his hand from my back and wrapped them around her waist.

"You know they're just for kitsch factor," he said, and his gaze stopped at her mouth. "They'll give you whatever you want."

She laughed with a tinkling, breaking crystal kind of sound. I felt as if I was chewing on the glass shards.

"Of course," she said with more than a loaded amount of silk in her voice. One that was saturated with intimacy. "But not everyone likes that scotch dishwater you drink, Maddox."

He eyed me with feigned indulgence. "Glenfiddich offends Kerri's Irish heart."

I stammered out something that sounded like how lovely and tried to get my feet to move in the direction of the queue and away from Maddox and his silky sounding date. Watching them fawn over each other was making me ill.

Scottie had disappeared, inside no doubt and up to no good involving that poor girl in his clutches. That left me open to find the queue and get inside.

I knew I needed to get about my own business. But for some reason, I felt like a failure already.

I braced myself with a deep inhale and headed toward the doorman, my initial confidence sagging even if my determination was renewed.

"We'll see you inside?" Maddox said from behind me.

I spun inelegantly in my shoes and tried to run a sophisticated smile over my features.

"My date is inside already," I said. "We have special access after the lecture. I doubt we'll have time to hang about and chit chat."

I kept my gaze on Kerri. Her eyes narrowed briefly at mention of special access. I mentally stabbed the air with a victory whoop.

Then she spoke and ruined it.

"There is no lecture," she said, indicating the real reason for her crestfallen look. Not jealousy at all. Annoyance, I discovered when she turned to Maddox. "You said I wouldn't have to sit through another boring history symposium."

She stabbed her finger into his chest. "You lied again," she said.

He curled his fist around her finger and pulled it down next to his side. There was a possessiveness to it that clogged up my throat.

"I did not lie," he told her softly, patiently. "I don't lie, and you know it."

She pulled away and threw her hip sideways, cocking her extricated hand along its slim curve. She was wearing Wang, I noticed, a deep black sheath so tarlike, it shimmered blue in the creases and made her tarry eyes look even more black. She looked like a goddess as she stood there.

Despite my determination to get back to business, I couldn't help watching them from the corner of my eye as I moved along in the line. A few other patrons seemed to think the same.

Kerri jerked her head in my direction.

"She said lecture." She said without looking at me.

"I agreed to a symposium," he pointed out with a cocky lift to his eyebrow. His voice, I noticed, had risen a decibel. "A lecture is a totally different thing."

She sniffed and hit him with her purse. Hard. Several people halted in their eddy toward the queue.

I caught my breath. This was a scene in the making. I needed to evade the exposure already melting down around the couple. I tried to move ahead a few people and got glared at for attempting to cut the line.

I settled for keeping my head down instead as she hit him again. He clutched at her wrists, whereupon she began kicking him with silver toed sandals.

I blinked stupidly and backed away, swinging my gaze left and right. More people had begun to rubberneck. A slim and wiry gentleman in a smart moss green suit broke away from the crowd nearest the doorman. Security alongside the doors squared their shoulders and lifted radio watches to their mouths.

Kerri began to complain loudly that Maddox never did anything she wanted, that he took her for granted. She was gorgeous and loud in her comments and that alone wouldn't make too much of a scene, but when she crossed into complaints about the bedroom, I knew there was no way to evade notice.

She threw in a complaint about him not being willing to engage in what she called lustful threesomes and then everyone who wasn't looking at them, swung their gazes their way, no doubt imagining exactly what she was detailing so perfectly and so specifically.

There was something breathtaking about the way she looked. Her hair came free of its sleek ponytail and wisped about her face. Her slim, graceful arms rose in the air as if dancing a frenzy.

The men in the crowds got smug, lustful looks as they watched her, and the women were running their eyes down Maddox's form with obvious sympathy and desire. I was rooted to the floor myself for a long moment, trapped by the image that cantered its way through my mind.

For the briefest of moments, I was wrapping naked legs over and between theirs and the sensation that rippled up my spine made me gasp.

I dropped my purse at the intensity of it.

I bent to retrieve my purse, grateful to duck out of sight. That was when I noticed, from the corner of my eye, the ruddy gentleman slip right past the doorman, whose eyes were on the gorgeous Kerri.

A distraction. That's what this was.

I should have seen it. Should have known it for what it was right away: nothing but a concerted and practiced means to get that green suited man past the guard.

It was a clichéd ploy but effective. With any other two people, it might not have worked, but they were both gorgeous. The addition of salacious detail made them impossible to resist. And the hole they left in the queue and in the attentions of the doorman made the perfect opportunity for the little man to slip by.

I should have felt irritation that someone else was here to work some mischief. Between Maddox and Scottie, there were all too many unknown plottings afoot. And they could serve only to make my own more complex and dangerous.

But all I could feel was relief. Maybe I didn't have to feel jealous of the gorgeous woman at all. In fact, she might be just the thing to have helped out my case. Who would look my way at all with her in the vicinity. Even Scottie would be hard pressed not to see her before any other woman.

I tried to convince myself of that as I rose and sidled my way through the crowds to the door that the relief was from the favor they'd done me by keeping my QR code intact and unused.

I felt that relief for all of three minutes before it all went to Hell.

CHAPTER 7

By the time I was inside, I was already grateful and had decided to push thoughts of both the gorgeous Kerri and the equally gorgeous Maddox out of my mind.

I had pinned my line of sight on the curator, standing alone with a smug look on his face as he surveyed the room. Servers brought trays of tall-stemmed glasses to patrons as they entered, and I shook my head as one of them, a middling height brunette with too heavy eyeshadow, offered a glass to me.

"Are you sure, hun?" she said. "This isn't the cheap stuff."

"I'm sure," I said with a thanks and tried to slip past her.

She sidestepped pretty effectively and blocked my escape. She pushed the tray toward me. She smelled of cheap perfume and for all the makeup, she still managed to look like a lesbian pretending to be straight. Her wrist was bruised where two small marks kissed against each other.

I found myself commenting on them despite my better judgement.

"Cat bite?" I said.

She twisted her wrist at my glance downward and shook her hand out. "Oh this," she said. "Damn cat. Got me in the leg too. You have any?"

"Cats?" I said to clarify. "One," I said, thinking about the feline who no doubt had already shredded my duvet in anticipation of my return.

"Match made in heaven, then," she said and cocked her hip at me. "We should drink to it."

Maybe she was paid by the glass, who knew. I plucked a stem from the tray and lifted it toward her. "*Slainte*," I said and made to lift it to my lips.

She smiled encouragingly. "I can get us a whole bottle for later, if you like."

This wasn't going well. She had already looked me over far too much for my comfort. Disguise be damned; too much exposure wasn't great either.

I started cursing my vanity in earnest. I never fancied myself overly attractive and perhaps had miscalculated the power of a ginger haired chick with her cleavage bared.

"Sure," I said, deciding hope was a lesser mnemonic than rejection. I searched out her name tag, thinking that at the very least, she might be useful. "Ismé, is it?"

"May," she said. "It's pronounced with a may at the end."

"Well Ismay," I said. "Sometimes gals gotta stick it to the man."

"Stick it to all men," she said as though she'd found a kindred spirit.

I smiled and lifted the glass again and let the bottom trail along the stem of my rose tattoo, pulling her eyes away from my face before spinning coyly around and hightailing it toward the curator.

He was still alone. Good. If I'd judged carefully, he'd be ordering the doors to the exhibition room open in about five minutes. My gaze skirted the lobby, eager to avoid Scottie's notice as I approached him.

Five minutes would be plenty of time for me to accost the curator with video of his unnatural proclivities and get through the exhibit room to the basement doors at the other end. While the rest of the party was enjoying a lecture and a bunch of dry-heaved pleadings for funding, I'd be picking through the crates in the basement and stashing a few priceless but miniature items.

I dropped my flute on a passing tray, mentally rubbing my palms together. My spine tingled the way it did when I was about to step into heist mode. So many variables. There was a certain excitement to it all.

An adrenaline junkie would love it.

I was no more than three feet away when I heard Scottie's voice and the chill he evoked chased the excitement down my spine, raising the downy hairs along the back of my neck. He was close. Maybe just a foot to my left.

I had the horrible thought that he'd know my scent, the way I stood. He'd seen me in disguise a good many times; he'd know me if I was dressed head to heel in a paper bag.

I stole a glance out the side of my peripherals. He was a foot away. But the girl stood between us, blocking his view of me and I might have been relieved at that, except her posture was off. Everything about her looked stiff and unnatural. Her demeanor screamed she wanted to be noticed.

And she was staring at me.

She was scared. Maybe even terrified. I totally got that. Scottie could have that effect on a person.

But I was not going to risk it. I had to tell myself that whatever he wanted from her, in the end, the room was full of people. He couldn't harm her outright. Whatever doom she was expecting, surely she had time to figure a way out of it. If she was smart.

But maybe she wasn't smart. Maybe she was just unfortunate.

Scottie collected those the most.

I groaned inwardly. It wasn't my problem. It couldn't be. I had to move on. Whatever trouble she was in she would have to work it out.

I turned my back toward them, angling so that he couldn't see my profile, only the lean of my shoulders.

The curator caught my eye. He was a man in his late 30s or early 40s, and he was handsome. The sort who looked like he sipped brandy or port after dinner. No one would suspect him of being a pedophile.

It amazed me the number of seedy folk in this city, but it always made for effective connections. If someone had a secret, they'd do anything to keep it, and you could work your way through a network of seedy folk without getting your hands dirty except for a bunch of proxy fingers.

But the pedophiles. I couldn't keep them around. I used them when I had to and discarded them as quickly as I could. They made me ill. And they were a bigger liability than I wanted.

So looking at the curator and the way he puffed out his chest as his patrons idled about drinking from champagne flutes and picking at Italian-style *cicchetti* morsels from the various trays, I knew he'd let me into the sanctum.

He'd give me those ten minutes because he needed to safeguard his reputation like a badger in his den.

I could be in and out in moments.

It was now or never.

I plastered a smile over my face and stuck my hand into my purse. I stepped toward him, pulling in a bracing breath.

Except that was when Scottie stepped forward too. Like lightening, the girl moved as well, funneling along with him toward me and the curator.

I knew right then what was happening. It was so clear. I'd been a fool to not see it before.

The girl was beautiful in an exotic way. Soft black hair, the blackest, inkiest of eyes.

And just the right age for the curator.

My stomach clenched into a fist of muscle.

Scottie was using that girl, and now I knew how.

My sense of indignation overcame me before my good sense could kick in. I took that last step and practically shoved the girl to the side. I think she might have stumbled. I didn't care.

All I wanted was to move her out of harm's way. I didn't notice until the curator yelped out loud that in my haste, I'd stepped on his toe.

His gaze landed on me, but instead of slipping to my cleavage where I'd spent so much care, it bit into my eyes.

I held my breath, hoping the expensive contacts would look real this close up. He glared at me for a long second before he repositioned his good natured, professional look onto his face.

"Mr. Mullens," I said, reading his name tag. "I'm looking forward to the symposium."

He extended his hand and nodded ever so slightly at me, obviously trying to reclaim his sense of professionalism.

I could feel eyes on my back, and I knew they were Scottie's. Whatever clump of rage had tightened my stomach had turned it into a rictus band of fear. But I was in for a penny now, time to peel off my pound of flesh and hope the circumstances would land later.

I reached for the curator's hand and used the contact to pull him toward me as I slid in close the way I'd seen Maddox's date do. I leaned in, whispering into the man's ear before he could recover his sense of surprise that a stranger would cuddle in so close.

"She's not for sale," I said, and he went tense beside me as he realized I wasn't coming on to him at all.

"I don't know what you're talking about," he said, angling his mouth toward my ear.

There was no time to be delicate or lengthy. I could feel Scottie moving in. The girl hovered beside me, obviously uncertain and too scared to move. I wished she'd back up some. She was making this more awkward than it already was.

"I have video," I said to the curator. "Don't ask what it has on it because you know. I want ten minutes in the basement. Alone. That's all."

He swung his eyes to mine. They were incredible to look at. I couldn't imagine him having to purchase company at all, except for the age he preferred and the sort of things I knew he did to them.

I doubted any woman would deny him anything with that skin, those lips, but he made me sick with anger as all those images flooded my mind.

The man was taking entirely too long, and I felt Scottie beside me, pressing closer. His aftershave spun all sorts of memories around me and my heart beat faster. I was a rabbit in a snare, waiting for him to pluck me free of the wire.

My heart hammered in my ears. I stared at the curator from the side of my eye, willing him to make the right decision.

Let me through. Just let me through.

"Ten," I clipped out. "And that man has to leave."

I ran my fingers along the back of his neck suggestively, wrapping my fingers around his throat the way I'd seen him do to a young girl. "Do it and I won't show anyone the Goldilocks and big bad bear show."

His gaze stabbed into mine and I had to work at not losing my nerve beneath the hatred in the gaze. My knees felt like they would require scaffolding to keep them up, but I smiled as though nothing unusual was happening. Just the way Scottie had taught me. Scottie who was already so close I could hear his breathing.

I wavered on my feet. He'd know. He'd know me. I needed to bolt.

But I stayed rooted to my spot. I had to.

I knew the curator was memorizing every detail of my face and clothes that he could before he nodded. Two slight bobs of his head that almost made me let go a hissing breath of relief.

I knew when he spoke, the words weren't for me, but the well dressed and groomed bull on my left.

"Your ticket," he said and held out his hand toward where I knew Scottie stood. "The doorman tells me it's fake."

I had to resist turning to face Scottie because I knew exactly what his face would look like and it was an expression that still haunted my nightmares. Handsome though it was, in fury, it held an equal amount of awe.

Something in my chest tightened with fear that he might have made me as he stood there so close, but I knew that if he had, he'd have plucked at my elbow with the same possessive authority he was used to with me.

I almost didn't breathe as I heard him complain that his ticket was as genuine as any other.

I kept my eye on the curator. "Am I good to go?" I prodded because he still hadn't nodded me through and I was as pinned to my spot as a moth to a board.

"Go," the curator said. "But someone comes in after you in 10:01."

I spun on my heel, feeling as though I'd narrowly missed getting struck by a double-decker bus.

I'd done it. Not two feet from Scottie and he hadn't made me. Not ten minutes more and I could be out of here, in the clear altogether.

I didn't take another breath until I could make out the individual beads in the curtain that separated the foyer from the exhibit room. Beyond that, the stairwell to the basement.

I was nearly there. The doorman lifted his walkie talkie to his mouth, nodded at me as I drew near. I pulled out my smartphone and tapped the timer.

I might have made it inside if someone hadn't grabbed me by the elbow and yanked me around so hard I nearly stumbled in my high heels.

Scottie. Minus the girl who clung to the side of the foyer door with wide eyes staring at the curator as though he were great mastodons about to stampede toward her. Maybe he was.

"Sis," Scottie said. "You look stunning."

CHAPTER 8

I TRIED NOT TO look at him, tried to see past him to the curator to see what the heck had happened. I didn't need to think to long to know that somehow Scottie's trump card was higher than mine. No. What I wanted to know was something more basic.

"How did you know it was me?" I asked him.

A long line of smirk threaded onto his mouth. "Your birth-mark."

I lifted my chin spitefully even as I mentally walked myself back through selecting the dress with the scooped back all the way to the crest of my buttocks.

"I don't have a birthmark," I said.

I knew exactly what mark he was talking about and I hadn't thought about it when I chose the dress because I'd been thinking about effect more than Scottie.

I hadn't thought about that one small half moon scar between my shoulder blades for a long time. It sat where he'd branded me after I'd run off with a bunch of girls to a down-town bar. It was an innocent outing, but I'd not told him I was going.

The overindulgence of booze did nothing to dampen the memory.

He leaned in close, letting his lips rest against my earlobe the way I had the curator. My heart tried to chisel its way free of my ribcage and I could swear he heard it and used it to bolster his ego.

"You were born for me the moment you were given to me," he whispered. "So whether it was natural or not, it is your birthmark."

I wanted to protest that I'd never been given. I chose him freely at first, thinking him dangerous and sexy. The girl in me had no idea what those things meant. The woman knew and she was still afraid.

I felt dizzy and if he hadn't still been holding onto my elbow and wrapped his arm around my waist, I might have staggered and lost my footing. I fleeted a look at the curator who had already moved from his spot toward the girl.

"How did you get him to let you stay?" I said, knowing it was futile to think my deal with the curator might still be good.

The doorman was already funneling people toward the curtain. A second guard headed straight through without hesitating. I had the feeling he'd pause at the door to the stairwell.

Scottie tugged me ever so gently away from the entry way as a crowd of people, eager to see the goodies, pressed closer.

I clutched at the beads behind me, knowing the opportunity was gone but not wanting to let go. All that work. Evaporated. And now I was in a worse spot than just losing the heist.

I should have left when I had the chance.

"You wear the dress well, Sis," he said pulling me against him. "I couldn't have picked it out for you better."

"You didn't answer my question," I said, laying a palm against his chest to keep from being pulled too close to him. His pecs felt like steel beneath his expensive suit and they tremored as my hand touched him.

He took my hand in his and pulled it down next to his thigh.

He thought I was checking for a gun and he didn't want me to find it. I nearly laughed out loud.

"Digital video is so easy to fake," he said then ran the pad of his thumb along my bottom lip. "And fingers are so difficult to replicate. Which would you elect to go with if it were you?"

The arm around my waist slid down and his hand sat low on my back so that it rested in the warm spot just above my buttocks. My whole body went clammy.

"You told him I was bluffing," I guessed.

"I told him we were having a lover's quarrel."

He shrugged and let a finger slip beneath my dress into the crevice where my cheeks joined, and I had to resist stomping on his foot because the last thing I wanted was to get tied now to whatever he was up to. Best I find a way to extricate myself without too much notice.

Scottie seemed oblivious to my temper and went on as though I hadn't gone rigid in his arms.

"He knew a lover's spat when he saw it," he said. "Lucky for me women can be so vindictive." He let go a restraining sigh. "No one wants to put up with that."

"Bastard," I said, fury doing its best to claw its way up my throat and dispel the sick taste of fear.

His eyebrow lifted delicately as though he'd heard the insult too many times to be bothered by it.

"You've met my mother," he said. "She wouldn't be pleased to hear you say that."

I needed a paper bag. I was either going to heave or pass out from hyperventilating. The pent-up frustration and adrenaline release was making me nauseated.

He tried to steer me toward the exhibit as though we were a couple who had come together, and I did my best to twist free. I could care less about the exhibit now, except for what he wanted from it. Or rather, what he planned to use that girl for.

"Stop wriggling," he commanded. "You'll cause a scene."

I caught sight of Maddox and his date eddying closer and remembered the little ruddy fellow who had obviously slipped in along with the scene they'd created. I wondered where he'd got to.

Maddox caught my eye and canted his head in a way that made me think he might share Scottie's thoughts about vindictive women.

I instantly stopped moving, and Scottie obviously thought it was the years of his careful conditioning.

"Better," he said and aimed me toward the door.

"What are you here for?" I said under my breath.

Scottie leaned close and nuzzled my cheek with his. "You, Sis. Why else?"

"Impossible," I said.

"Not so impossible. What's impossible is you thinking you have connections that I don't."

"You're saying you baited me here."

He shrugged. "I'm saying the job you think you're here for is a dud. There is no uncatalogued cache." He chuckled. "But it's the kind of thing you love, and I knew it would bring you out into the open."

"Bastard," I said again, eying Maddox and his date as they showed their tickets to the doorman and were ushered in along with several dusty seniors who wore the distinct look of money the way most people wore expression.

I hadn't been overly curious about Maddox's presence at first, the same as Scottie's because both of them had connections and interests the same way I did. I'd taken for granted that they wanted something, that their presence was not coincidence, even if it made things more difficult for me.

But Maddox was from the other world too. He'd told me he dealt in only the rarest of things. Not your grandmother's pearls, he'd said to me once.

Suspicion crept its way up my spine. I looked at Scottie a bit closer. His sandy colored hair was greased back, all the better to show his square jawline. He looked shorter than his normal height in a suit that bulged out across his shoulders.

He could afford a better fitting suit than that, and I knew it. No doubt he had on a second, more suitable for running, outfit on underneath.

"How did you get away from Finn?" I said.

He squeezed me tight to him at the same moment Maddox and his date stepped through the curtain and he threw a look back at me. I tried not to wilt under the scrutiny.

"Finn?" Scottie said. "Who's Finn?"

He shuffled me along with him as the doorman held his walkie talkie to his mouth and spoke into it. A crackle of sound came through and he nodded at Scottie.

"Oh my God," I said as we pushed through the curtain without so much s showing a ticket. "He's in on it too." I imagined what those two rogues would do with the girl once the party was over. "That poor girl."

Scottie sighed. "What are you talking about?" he said. "I paid him well, so we might as well enjoy ourselves don't you think?"

I tried to pull my arm from his grip and he glared down at me as we crossed the threshold.

The room was more expansive than I realized, but it was already filled with people. Every part of the exhibit was cordoned off by velvet ropes several feet away. Small and large alike, they sent the message that the artifacts were not to be touched.

Perhaps most of the company wouldn't notice the small lasers installed on the poles that held the ropes, but I noticed them.

Scottie tightened his grip on my back as we passed by a tall white pillar shaped very much like a human woman. Crystals embedded in the stone winked in the light that caught the curves.

The chandeliers that lined the center of the room had been dimmed and a champagne fountain on the other end made sure to beckon the suited and gowned patrons toward the lecture podium.

I heard Kerri groan out loud when she saw that the lecture would be given to a standing crowd.

"So," I pressed. "How did you manage to slip away from him?"

"Who?" he said, distracted as we drew close to a plinth with a single artifact light from every side. A coin of some sort, I thought, faced with what looked like electrum. "You mean that guy I sold those ridiculous mosaic tiles to?"

My heart lurched. Sold. Finn had refused to pay me for mine.

Scottie chuckled. "What an idiot. Took him for everything he had. I knew the things were valuable, but he acted like they were priceless."

"So you grifted him," I said, but I suspected differently.

The Finn I'd met would have just killed them all and be done with it. I'd banked on it, in fact. If Scottie was hale and hearty and believed he'd made a small fortune, then no doubt Finn had done something magical to his memory.

Lucky for Scottie, he'd been left alive to believe he'd scored big-time. Unlucky for me.

At that, Scottie leaned toward the electrum coin, pulling me with him. "Beautiful isn't it?" he said under his breath.

I peered at the plush cushion the coin sat on. "Look all you want," I said. "There's no way you can steal it now."

He chortled. "Oh, Sis," he said. "Still the small-time heist mind." He adjusted his sleeve cuffs beneath his jacket.

"You have no interest in it?" I said. "Honestly."

Those lips I'd once believed sensual thinned out as he smiled lazily. "You're the treasure I came for, Sis. Give me ten minutes and I'll prove it to you."

Ten minutes. With my own job already in the toilet, and his clutch on me so tight, I knew whatever freedom I had was on a short leash. I needed to abort and abort now.

"I need to find the loo," I said. "Before the curator takes the podium. I don't want to miss the lecture."

"No worries," he said. "There won't be a lecture."

"Well, I need to go."

"What's the rush, Sis?" He squeezed me into his side, where I felt the gun he'd thought I'd been searching for earlier. It poked into my ribcage. A Ruger by the feel of it.

With the heels I was about his height and I knew that would make him feel off. He was used to looking down on me. I pasted a coy smile on my face.

"A gal has some modesties," I said.

He wasn't to be fooled.

"Take care of it later in the hotel."

The tone was brusque, and I knew there was no way he was letting me go. He nodded to two men who flanked the doorway and their eyes fell on me. One of them grinned at me. Alvin. The muscle who had bought me a latte all those weeks ago.

He strolled amiably toward the other end of the hall where a second door no doubt led out into other exhibits and then out a back door.

Effectively cutting off both of my retreats.

I started to panic.

Then the lights went completely out, and everything went deadly black. I jumped and knocked my head into Scottie's. I tasted blood.

And the panic really bloomed then, right on the heels of a sudden fruitless thought that the dark could afford me cover to run.

Except a flash of light beside me, small, but unmistakable, bit into the dark and took a chunk out of my thigh. The sound of the electrical jolt came second, along with that of my dress tearing.

The next sound was a scream.

CHAPTER 9

I WAS SURPRISED TO hear the scream was my own, and that it was being punctuated by a room full of equally panicked shrieks filled with pain and surprise. Lights flashed all over the room, igniting the faces of scared women for a brief second before going dark and finding another.

Strobes, I realized. They made each movement seem disjointed and dizzying. But they couldn't account for the shocks that struck every now and then, eliciting startled yelps.

The tension in the room was as electric as those shocks. I could hear what I assumed were guards mobilizing at the door.

I ran the back of my forearm across my mouth, thinking to clear it of the blood I must have spilled when I'd bit my tongue. I felt nothing.

"What are you doing?" I asked Scottie, feeling him next to me in the dark. "And how are you doing it?"

He grabbed my hand, obviously thinking correctly that given the chance, I'd bolt.

"What am I doing?" he growled. "Not a goddamn thing."

I felt his agitation. It was far more palpable than the electricity surging through the room in bite-sized pieces and in between blackouts. Whatever was happening, he wasn't at the heart of it, and it was no doubt ruining his own plans.

"This isn't you," I said and even as the words came out, I knew who was to blame.

Maddox.

"Not me," he said, and he sounded about as pissed as I'd ever heard him. "And not you either, I'm guessing."

I squeaked as I felt someone brush against me, a little too close and unexpected.

Scottie wrapped his arms around me and pulled me into his chest, protectively to the casual observer who might catch sight of it during the brief flashes of light.

I knew better. What often seemed protective was most usually possessive.

"You're smothering me," I complained into his chest and ran my hands up along his ribcage. The gun was there somewhere. I just needed to get my hands on it.

A snapping sound cracked through the air on my left side, halting my hands just as another flash of light lit Scottie's face. I watched it like a static shock sizzle into his cheek. He bellowed in rage just as my hand found his gun.

It was right about that moment that whoever had brushed against me actually took hold of my elbow and yanked.

Hard.

I peeled away from Scottie's grip with the gun still in my hand. I swung around blindly, raising the pistol toward whoever had hold of me. The thug, no doubt. I might thank him for ripping me loose from Scottie, but he'd taste a bit of metal if he thought I was going with him.

"Back off," I growled. "Or I'll shoot."

"Sis?" Scottie said from somewhere to my right. I balked. He sounded afraid.

He couldn't see me. I couldn't see him. The room was blacker-than-should-be black. I could hear my own breathing.

I could hear everyone's breathing as they waited for another blast of light or for the chandeliers to sizzle to life or for the guards to do something.

Because no one was doing anything except no doubt standing frozen to their spots in shock and fear.

I tried in vain to see through the dark. My eyes felt as though they were too wide and yet nothing, no shape nor form revealed itself through the shadows. I minced sideways, hoping the thug couldn't see me either.

"Put it down," said a voice.

Maddox. Right in front of me.

Scottie heard it too. "Sis?" he said. "I'm right here, babe. Talk to me."

Like hell I would. The same hell I'd put my weapon down for. In this dark, where I had no idea who was friend or foe, I would put it down when I fell.

I took a step forward, aiming for what I hoped was the exit and bumped into the velvet rope. I ran my fingers along the cording.

The coin. The electrum coin. Whoever was responsible for the blackout and the frenzy of the guards as they worked to herd everyone out of range of the valuables had no doubt come for the coin. It was small. It was pocketable. No one had found me yet. There weren't nearly enough guards to get everyone back from everything or herded into he next room.

I didn't have pockets, but I had a purse. I felt my way along the cord to the plinth. My fingers were roaming the top of it, rubbing along the velvet.

They were a hair's breadth away from the coin itself.

A voice hissed in my ear.

"Don't touch it," it said.

I made for one final grab, but I was tugged backward by broad hands into Maddox's chest. The smell of smoke and aftershave surrounded me.

"It's hers," he said in my ear. "Leave it be."

He had hold of my wrists, and the gun dropped to the floor with a thud.

"He's looking for you," Maddox said in an urgent tone that made me think he could see through the dark and right through to Scottie's soul. "Should he find you?"

"No." The words were wrenched from me as I thought of how close I'd come to being Scottie's bitch again.

The lights fizzled the way they do when power is struggling to come back online. I got a brief glimpse of Maddox at my side, of Scottie catching sight of me and eating up the distance with brisk, determined strides, before everything went black again.

The dying of the light sent a few more images to my cortex: armed guards, flashlights and rifles in hand, rushing in through the doors and herding the crowd like sheep.

Someone cursed, unaware that what was happening was more important than a few power outages.

"He's coming," Maddox hissed and I quailed, trying to decide which way to bolt in the dark.

"Which way?" I said, frantic now.

"Quiet," he said, as rough hands, Maddox's I told myself, shoved me sideways. His body shielded me from the back. I felt him there, towering above me even in my heels and then he began pressing closer forcing me to inch along awkwardly.

Why were the flashlights not working? What was happening?

I stumbled. My hands flew forward to catch myself as I spilled onto the floor and I thudded against the tiles with a jolt to my wrists. I managed to bite back a curse as the hot pain made a lightening trail up to my elbow.

I felt my left breast come free of the dress and I scrabbled about, trying to get up again.

Someone in heels trampled on my fingers and I did cry out then, unable to hold back the note of pain. I heard Scottie call out to me, anxiety in his voice. He wanted to know where I was. Was I okay? Talk to me, Sis. Let me know where you are.

The young Isabella might have felt pity at the sound of it, wanted to soothe his worry. Now, all I could do was crawl in the opposite direction of that voice, fumbling around in the dark as I tried to escape. I heard the distinctive sound of my dress tearing and a draft of air met the backs of my thighs.

Great.

"For fuck's sake," Maddox said from above me, and next I knew I was being scooped up beneath the knees and behind my shoulders, cradled against his chest.

I considered protesting at the indignity of it, but in the end, I didn't care how I got away from Scottie, so long as I got away. I ended up clinging on tight like Whitney Houston in the *Bodyguard* and urging him to hurry the hell up.

Not very damsel-like in the end judging by the way he eyed me at with every curse I let go.

I didn't care about that either.

He shouldered his way through the darkness in what I hoped was the right direction. Different fragrances of after-shave, soap, and perfume pervaded the air. Someone elbowed me in the head. I heard the walkies snapping on and off with clipped statements. No power outages in the city. Isolated to the museum. The breakers were all intact.

Alarms started ringing, shrill and demanding and several of the women screamed again. It finally dawned on them that this was no ordinary brownout. It was intentional.

No doubt the museum was already on lockdown and there were police everywhere outside. Every exit, every air duct and crevice being guarded or scoured through. No one would get out without coming under scrutiny first.

Double great.

"Don't worry, Kitten," Maddox said as though I'd telecasted my thoughts to him, and maybe the way I tensed up did just that. "You didn't steal anything, did you?"

No. I hadn't. I was a mere patron of history tonight thanks to Scottie. Despite how the evening began, I hadn't used any of the tools I'd brought, and I hadn't lifted or grifted one thing.

Somehow that didn't make me feel better.

"Just a little more," he said. "We're almost there."

I was about to ask what he meant when a voice sounded to my right, addressing Maddox, apparently, by the intimate way it sounded.

"He's got it," Kerri said.

"Good," Maddox said. "Now we can get the hell out of here."

He picked up his pace and managed to avoid the guards I knew were still floundering and trying to empty the room.

I didn't question why until the lights suddenly flooded the room again and I could see we were inches from the door, that two guards who stood beside it were smacking their flashlights against their palms, till they suddenly swam into full working order.

They looked so bewildered at the light that I wondered if they thought some magic had befallen every light in the building.

Maybe it had. In fact, I was sure of it.

"Is this you?" I hissed against his ear.

He knew better than to try and con me. "The blackouts, yes, but the light show? No. Some elemental power. Which is why we need to get out of here."

As though that was some sort of signal, Maddox dropped me to the floor and I had to clutch at him to keep from falling. I'd lost a shoe and was unsteady on my feet.

His gaze dropped to the rose stem between my breasts as he steadied me, and I scrabbled to find the edge of my dress to pull it closed. I flushed with heat from heel to hair when I realized he hadn't been looking at the rose at all, but at the bared breast that had come free during the scuffle.

He aimed me gently toward the curtain without so much as mentioning my awkward state of undress, but I noted his eyes didn't lift to my face until he spoke.

"Better run, little kitten," he said and tossed a look over his shoulder. "Your lover looks awfully pissed."

Scottie did look pissed. But he was too far from the exit to do anything once a guard noticed him standing a little too close to the plinth where I'd been just seconds earlier.

Kerri made a small sound of amusement from beside me and I assumed it was for Scottie's decidedly furious glare in our direction until she adjusted my dress along my backside and patted the skirts into place. The draft of cold air cut off, indicating I'd been showing a lot more than a bared breast.

I simmered in quiet humiliation and felt like a filthy urchin despite her careful touch-ups. I looked up at her as she averted her gaze from the obvious tear along the back seam toward Scottie who was now being manhandled into handcuffs and away from the plinth.

"I wonder why that young man would be so foolish to steal something right under their noses," she sniffed.

She regarded Maddox with a lifted silver brow. "Not brash, but rather stupid, don't you think?"

I stared at the plinth at her words. The coin was gone.

CHAPTER 10

KERRI PEERED DOWN AT me as I clutched the pieces of torn dress together over my breast. I felt decidedly silly under that scrutiny, especially the way she'd called Scottie young despite looking at least half a dozen years younger than he was.

"You best run along," she said. "Before folks begin to remember seeing you with him."

"I wasn't--"

"Go," Maddox barked at me and I immediately responded.

He fell into step behind me out through the swept aside curtain meant to separate the exhibit from the foyer and into a handful of security guards patting down patrons as they emerged.

The general state of confusion and chaos didn't lift from the foyer as I stepped across the threshold to a room filled with angry, confused, and upset patrons. Someone complained rather loudly that she hadn't got to see the mummy.

I searched the room for the curator and found him with his jaw clenched, the teenager hovering next to him. Her eyes looked strangely calm despite the terror they showed just moments earlier. Maybe she thought she'd been reprieved.

She locked gazes with me and held mine for several moments before jerking her head toward the exit. Meet me, that movement said. I flicked my gaze to the curator as rough hands pulled me aside and patted me down.

He looked mightily put out and I was beginning to understand why. Through the glass doors and wall of windows that showed the street outside, I could see the city fully lit and the sidewalks crammed with security and looky-loos.

The museum had been targeted all right, and judging by the missing coin, the handcuffs snapped on Scottie's wrists, and the presence of what looked like plainclothes dicks, it had been successful.

Don't touch it, Maddox had said. *It's hers.*

I had no idea how that coin could have been Kerri's, but I knew it was. Just as I knew the little ruddy fellow was in her employ and the scene out front had been a distraction.

I looked over my shoulder for Kerri, feeling a bit more relaxed with Scottie out of sight. She didn't look guilty. Rather, she was busy querying those around her what they thought was going on. Maddox stood like a mannequin next to her.

And that too was a setup.

I wanted to let him know I knew exactly what was going on, but he whistled for the guard who was running everyone who wanted out, through some sort of security check before they could leave the museum.

"She's a bit of a mess, I'm afraid," he said of me to the guard. "Got trampled in there."

He looked angrily at the exhibit room. "The museum's negligence is appalling. She needs to go home now before I decide to press charges."

I was about to protest at the way he called me a mess, but he stepped up to the guard, towering over him. "Check her out now. She's embarrassed enough."

He snapped his suit jacket cuffs down and gave the impression that if the guard didn't do as asked, there would be hell to pay. And the guard, for whatever reason, was perfectly happy to be ordered about. I might have figured it had more to do with my bedraggled state, except he wasn't even looking at my cleavage.

He was staring at Maddox.

I looked Maddox over, trying to see if he had some sort of inhuman compulsion, but all he did was look back down at me with something like compassion and it made my heart stutter, the damn thing.

I was about to protest that I didn't want to be patted down the way the others were enduring, but the guard ran light hands down over my legs and torso. I eyed his handheld detector that he kept at his side, that by all rights he should have used, expecting it to come into play at any moment. It didn't.

He made me empty my purse. I chewed my lip quietly until he passed over the QR code ticket and jerked his head toward the door.

I couldn't wait to get out of there.

Maddox snagged my arm, holding me back.

He peeled off his suit jacket and laid it over my shoulders. It was big enough that it would cover my backside and could wrap almost double over my midriff.

He flashed a grin at me. "Not that it's not a good show, mind you, but there's already too much here to see."

He turned back to the guard, lifting his arms out to the sides so the detector could run him up and down. I turned heel to see Alvin clenching his fists as he waited in line. I'd forgotten about him.

Apparently, he hadn't forgotten about me.

I fled the museum the way a criminal flees the scene. I'd been reprieved no matter which way I sliced it. The problem was, I'd also lost any chance at making any money, lost the weeks of prep. Hell, I'd even lost the chance to leave the place with my dignity intact.

I was hailing an Uber two blocks away when I heard the sound of someone creeping through bushes and dried up foliage. Alvin, undoubtedly. Or the other thug.

I had no gun, no protection. I was in heels for heaven's sake in a dress that was in tatters and couldn't run.

So I did what I could.

I swung around with my cell phone flash blazing out into the dark street.

Nothing.

Not one person stood on the sidewalk. No dog. No rat. No cat. Nothing but the city planted trees with their lush foliage interfering with the light form the streetlamps.

But I knew I'd heard something and I regretted taking a quiet street instead of running headlong down the main thoroughfare. If Alvin had followed me, I was as good as done for.

He'd yank me back to Scottie and when the police released him--because they would--there'd be no getting away this time. There was no Finn or magic rune to save me.

I backed away, scanning the trees and darker alleys. A breeze came up and whispered through the leaves. I pulled the jacket tighter.

"If you're coming for me, you piece of shit, then don't keep me waiting."

It sounded half brave, I thought. Maybe he'd buy it.

I panned the light from my phone over the garbage cans and into the shadows, walking backward the whole time. I half expected to bump into my assailant the way things like that happened in movies, so when my light fell on the teenaged girl from the museum, I jumped nearly out of my skin.

"What the hell?" I said, irritated because she'd scared the bejesus out of me for nothing. I hissed out a relieved sigh.

She emerged from the shadows behind a tree and stood out in the middle of the sidewalk with her head cocked to the side. Her hair hung loose and seemed to knot itself into long dreadlocks. She blinked at me. Long, languid movements of her eyelids that had to be impossible unless she was zoned out on drugs. If not, then one word and one word only fit the way she stood there.

Creepy.

A shit ton of strange things had happened throughout the evening, but none of them made my skin crawl the way it did from the girl just standing there. Traumatized, I thought. How long had she been with Scottie? Held and saved till just the right moment to exploit when it suited him?

I might have believed it readily, except children didn't necessarily fit into Scottie's usual methodology. He'd not allowed me to enter his true circle until I was older, and I'd watched dozens of women come and go in his greater circle. But he'd never taken on children before.

Despite the careful grooming he did with all his women, they all fit a certain pattern: poor, beautiful, intimacy issues. He took them under his wing when they were most vulnerable and even sent some to college or university, gaining trust and a sense of debt. Many of them quietly invaded organizations he had targeted as useful.

This was different. New. And it meant a whole new level of danger if the man I knew was ready to use pre-adults the way he'd used the girl at the museum.

It made me anxious for the girl. What was Scottie after that he was grooming children for?

"Are you alright?" I asked her, caught between wanting to help her out, and knowing Scottie might have sent her.

I paused as I stepped forward. What if this was a trap?

"Are you real?" she said.

The way she said it made the hairs on my arms stand up beneath Maddox's jacket. A shiver went down my spine. This girl was no young innocent. I would bet my cat on it.

If my uber hadn't pulled up right then I might have demanded more of an explanation. As it was she took one look at the SUV and then threw a look back over her shoulder and stepped behind the tree. I shook my head to clear the cobwebs. The driver rolled down the passenger window.

"Are you getting in?" he said.

I yanked the door open and slid inside. I couldn't pull the door closed fast enough.

I stared out the window, watching the buildings blur by, trying to work out what it was that Scottie had been after. He'd been at the museum for a reason, used that girl as a decoy when he never used children that way. As bad as he was, he had his limits. And then there was the girl herself. The flickering of the lights that Maddox claimed was not due to anything he'd planned.

As a puzzle, it ranked right up there.

I was too tired to walk too far, so I got the driver to drop me off one street down from the brownstone instead of the usual four or five. Maybe just this once I could forgo the exhausting walk. I was cold and in tatters. Creeped out and in need of a locked door.

A quick glance left and right told me I was safe to head in, but I hesitated.

The building looked like it always did to me in the dark. There was a small garden out front that my landlord kept wild and in disarray. The overgrown clumps of flowers and foliage were well within the bylines because he kept it weeded, but it was messy, and his neighbors hated messy.

Even in the faint illumination of a too weak porch light I could see a newly formed spider web clinging to the stem of a fading poppy.

I sighed and went in, wondering the whole time if I was crossing into the fae warlord's realm as I walked through my front door or if he'd already taken off the glamor and I was returning to an apartment I'd not set foot in for weeks.

My answer came when the cat didn't streak across the apartment at me, all hiss and raised fur. As guard dogs went, she was pretty decent.

"Seriously?" I said, dangling my heels by their straps in my hand as I stood in the bedroom doorway. The bastard took off the glamor all right, but he'd left my cat back in his realm.

I strode to the kitchen counter and noticed a shard of glass embedded in the grout of the floor. I bent to stick my finger to it and discard it.

Obviously the fae warlord had been taunting me and the glass had indeed broken in my apartment, which meant all kinds of ridiculously impossible things were going on here whenever something happened in the fae realm version.

I tried to imagine glasses sailing through the air on their own toward the fridge as I poured a glass of milk, dishes washing themselves, laundry being sorted and put away.

The stress and adrenaline release had me chuckling over the stupidity of it all and I sank down onto the floor with my legs splayed in front of me. Maddox's jacket hung from my shoulders and the thought of that for some reason made me cry.

Which is exactly the state Alvin found me in.

CHAPTER 11

I WAS SHOCKED TO see him standing in my living room, looking across the open space to my kitchenette, but there he was. I
didn't ask how he got in or how he'd found me. The warlord's
specific glamor was off, and I'd taken a short cut because the
night was a clusterfuck and I didn't have it in me to be careful.

He'd found me the way anyone would. Followed me and
stepped right through the front door because I'd forgotten to
lock it.

He wore a smirk like the bad suit he had on and he took off
that cheap jacket so leisurely, I knew before he spoke what he'd
come for.

"Scottie sent you to collect me," I said, hoping that was all it
was.

Alvin rolled up first one, then the other sleeve, before apparently deciding that wouldn't be enough and took his shirt
off right off. He was hairy enough, but not as covered as I'd
expected. I'd thought before that he was pudgy, an overstuffed
brute who ate too many danish and used his size instead of
muscle to intimidate.

I was wrong. The muscles under his wife beater shirt moved
as though they were hard chunks of steel. There was no life,
no fluidity to them at all. No lithe movement like a cheetah or
lion's big working muscles.

They were hard blocks of cement beneath his skin.

I tried and failed to stand and had to roll over onto my knees to get to my feet. And I knew I needed to get to my feet. Quickly.

The blow to my cheekbone sent me straight back down to the floor before I could weave away or stand straight. I couldn't see the floor tiles for the black spots in my vision.

"Scottie sent me to teach you a lesson," he said. "And he told me to make sure you learned it."

There was glee in his tone, too much glee to make me think the lesson would be a quick one.

I turned my face toward him, looking up at him as he loomed above me.

I held up my hand, thinking maybe he would halt long enough for me to explain or protest.

He didn't. The blows came again, this time in more targeted areas: my stomach, ribs, and then finally my face. I'd thought perhaps for Scottie's vanity's sake, I would be spared my face.

My nose crunched, and pain ripped into my skull.

If I whimpered he didn't hear it. His steel-toed shoes went into my ribs next until I curled into a fetal position, vainly trying to protect my core.

It went on for too long. The lesson was a long, painful, pointed one and long after he'd stopped hitting me, I still felt the blows. My cell memory wasn't sure whether it was Alvin's fists or Scottie's, and I supposed they were one and the same, after all.

The last thing I remembered before blacking out was Alvin looking over his shoulder at me as he stood at the open doorway.

"You know where he's staying," he said with his hand on the doorknob. "Your hall pass expires in twenty-four hours."

It was clever, that quip. Far smarter than I gave Alvin credit for. I had time to think I really needed to reconsider how cunning he was.

And then I did black out. Merciful, painless unconsciousness and when I woke again, it was to birdsong.

I tried to roll over, thinking I was in bed at first and was just confused about why my mattress was so damn stiff.

When pain flared through my ribcage, I remembered exactly where I was and why.

I was on my kitchen floor. I hurt like hell. And I had probably twelve hours or so to deliver myself to my ex-lover or risk worse than a few punches and kicks.

I managed to squirm onto to my back, but it left me huffing and trying to hold my ribcage together beneath the suit jacket I still wore. It snagged by a button to a hank of my hair, reminding me exactly how much my scalp hurt.

I vaguely remembered why that was too. Something about Alvin grabbing me by the hair and dragging me several feet toward the door in a threat to haul me all the way to the jail where Scottie was being held for twenty-four hours because of me.

But he'd given up and spun me right back around and dumped me next to the sink so I could splash my face with water if I needed to.

He had his orders, after all.

I bit him, if I remembered correctly. One great chomp out of a hunk of muscled calf because it was the only thing I could reach from my spot on the floor.

It was foolish. It had escalated what had no doubt meant to be a brief but brutal reminder into an all-out rage fest.

I quivered all over as my memory tried to bring every moment back to bear, and the instinct of self-preservation forced it back in. Like a jar that refused to have is lid screwed shut, I kept having to retract and refit, and the effort made me tremble. I leaked frustrated tears onto my cheek.

I couldn't cry. It hurt too much. Salty fluid ran into the corner of my mouth and stung.

I tasted blood.

And the taste of copper in my mouth yanked a sob out me finally because it reminded me of why I was in this mess in the first place. I should have listened to the fae warlord. What would it have cost me, after all? A few bones and a nest of vampires? What was that to the beating I'd just endured?

I let go. No matter that it hurt every part of my body to do so, I let go lying on my back with my arms flung out because I couldn't even curl into the fetal position.

I wasn't sure how long I lay there that way. I knew something caught my attention only through the near-silent wailing. I hitched the tears back down, swallowing greasy saliva as I tried to make out what had tweaked my senses.

Alvin wouldn't have knocked. Neither would Scottie.

Except I didn't even know if it was a knock I'd heard in the first place.

I tried and failed to roll over onto my side. I had to settle for letting my head roll toward the door.

A sharp intake of breath was the thing I did register. That and the sound of shoes scuffing across the floor toward me.

I thought I heard my name.

I cringed in reflex and tried to scrabble to my feet, thankful that terror has a way of overriding pain in the worst circumstances. I had a gun in my bedroom. Half a dozen knives in the kitchen drawer. A broken bottom of glass I could use to stab at whoever came at me.

Any one of them would do in a pinch.

A hand clamped down over my wrist as I went for the drawer and I whirled around in a flat-out panic, seeing nothing but a sizable chest and the blur of color. My eyes, I realized. I could barely see through them. I couldn't even open them.

"Sweet Jesus, Kitten," the intruder said. "Who the fuck did this to you?"

Maddox. Maddox was the one in my apartment. Not Alvin. Not Scottie.

I sagged against the counter. Not Scottie. Not Alvin. I shouldn't have felt safe knowing that Maddox had let himself in to my apartment, an apartment that was now painfully accessible to rabble and friends alike.

And yet I did feel safe.

So why did I yank my hand back so violently from his? Why did I pull it into my chest as though I couldn't risk letting any part of myself be out in space, vulnerable and accessible?

"Don't touch me," I said in a voice that couldn't possibly be my own. It was too high pitched, too shrill. I felt my head shaking back and forth. A renewed sting of tears made my eyelids hurt.

"Ok," he murmured. "I won't touch you. Can you walk? Can you make it to the sofa?"

His voice was all soft and soothing and I hated that I responded to it because it made me feel even more weak.

Even so, I nodded. Except the truth was, I had no idea if I could walk. I felt like a bunch of frayed wires all bundled together, but with open sores where critical electricity leaked out.

Soaked through and through with adrenaline and fear, my memory flashed me back to the night I'd left Scottie and run from him in my bare feet and hid out in a ditch for hours.

I swore then I would never go back to him. I swore I'd die before he controlled me again.

And I think I almost did just that.

I couldn't even hug myself to keep the shakes from rattling my teeth. They clacked together like a joke set and I expected someone somewhere to laugh. I took a step in the direction of the sofa and nearly collapsed.

Maddox made a grab for me, assuming I was about to fall but I slapped his hand away.

"My apartment," I said.

My apartment. My walls. My sofa. I knew where everything was in the dark; I could find the sofa with a bruised and swollen eye.

"OK," he said again but I could feel him hovering over me as I hand-walked my way along the counter and then wall to find the arm of my sofa.

"Right here," I said as I found the seat with my palms. "This is where he sat."

"Bastard," said Maddox and I eased onto the cushions, aiming my face to where his voice had come from. He thought I meant Alvin. He had no idea about the fae warlord.

I could feel him standing there. He hummed with fury as I tried to find a comfortable way to sit without hurting my bruised legs. The blur of color that was his shirt and trousers moved silently away from me.

I heard a tap squeak on and then running water splashing into my bathroom sink. He came back after several moments and dabbed ever so gently at my eyelids.

I cursed at the first touchdown of the warm, wet cloth on my raw eyelids.

"Sorry," he said, but he didn't stop. His touch was gentle and when I was able to brace myself, relieving. I had no idea how much gunk had gummed up my eyelids until I could see him more clearly.

His face was inches from mine as he knelt in front of me.

And the expression was murderous.

My gaze dropped to the cloth, a favorite one I'd stolen from a hotel when I'd first run from Scottie. It had been thick and lush and white. A perfect metaphor for the life I wanted to live. A fresh start.

Now it was coated in clotted blood.

"Oh my God," I said.

"Yeah."

Not just tears and sweat had coated my eyelids closed, but blood. And lots of it. I didn't want to touch my face. I had the feeling my cheekbone was double its size, maybe even cracked.

I clutched at the sofa cushions on either side of me, trying my best not to break down in front of him. I could hear my breath coming in hitching gasps as I began to hyperventilate.

The murderous expression disappeared and in its place a sort of calm, compassionate one.

"Don't," I said.

"Don't what?" he said. "Don't let you know someone cares?"

I shook my head. I had no idea what I meant except that I was dangerously close to losing my shit and I had no idea what the trigger would be or how it would look or what I would do. My hold on my control was as thready as the cushions I was clutching at.

"I promised I wouldn't touch you, but I'm retracting that," he said in a gruff voice and before I could consent or deny, he ran the back of his hand down the length of my hair.

My scalp hurt where his fingers landed. Something caught on his thumb. A knot. Or a clump or tangle.

"I'm going to clean you up," he said. Not a request. Not an order either. Something in between.

I nodded, and he made a small grunting noise. I watched him retreat to the bathroom and heard the shower turn on.

I looked down at my hands. They were unmarked and clean. I turned them over. Not a single mark on them.

I ran my fingers through my hair and they stuck on a snarl. A wet snarl.

I hoped it was fluid from my nose and not blood. Please God, don't let it be blood.

I told myself I would not look, but of course, I did.

CHAPTER 12

I NEARLY FAINTED WHEN I saw the amount of gore on my hand from running them over my hair. Snot, yes, but blood too, although much less than I thought.

"Looks like he spat on you," Maddox said in a deadpan voice and I realized while I was staring at my hands, he had come back into the room and was standing in front of me.

All the way from the bathroom and I hadn't heard him move.

I looked up at him stupidly. I couldn't form any words.

He held a hand out to me.

"Come," he said. "It's warm and ready."

I just stared.

He sighed then stooped to help me to my feet. Like a lamb being led, I went with him to the bathroom. I stood woodenly as he stripped me gently down to my panties. He kept his eyes on my face, but what was in his was unreadable.

I realized I was still wearing the dress only when he wadded it up and threw it in the trash. My expensive dress. The one I looked so good in. I sucked in a breath and would have bit down on my lip if the thickness of it didn't remind me how much that would hurt.

I could hear my apartment-sized dryer rolling around half-full. It hummed quietly above the stacked washer as steam billowed about us.

My mirror had been covered over by a towel and everything around us smelled faintly of lavender and peppermint. He'd put on my infuser. That small act made me want to whimper.

"Come now," he said and eased me into the shower.

The water sprayed around me, but he was careful to position me out of the direct spray, instead wetting my natural sponge and squeezing it out over my skin.

He didn't so much as touch me. The sponge never met flesh. He just sluiced warm water over me until the blood and snot ran down the drain. I watched it go without emotion. He turned me back-to, careful to tug my panties up where the water was bogging them down.

His arms came around me slowly, cautiously as he reached for the shampoo bottle on the ledge. I knew he was making slow, deliberate movements not to scare me and I imagined he was getting soaked from the back spray.

The bottle made a spurting noise as he squeezed soap into his palm. The scent of coconut and papaya met my nose as he retracted his arms just as slowly as he'd reached in.

He massaged my scalp delicately where it didn't hurt and skirted the section that did as though he knew exactly where the pain was. One gentle turn and my back was to the spray. He tilted my head back, cradling my nape so it didn't strain.

He was gentle. So gentle. Those large, calloused hands of his brushed against my cheek once and I winced, but other than that, I felt nothing.

After he shut the water off, he disappeared for several seconds. The door to the dryer opened and closed. He appeared in my line of vision again, holding out a bath towel.

"Come to me," he said and when I did he wrapped the warmth of the hot towel around me.

"You've done this before," I croaked out. "Showered with women."

"I've been in the same shape before," he said, careful to keep his eyes chastely on mine.

I nodded, not sure what to say to that.

"Will you let me look at you?" he said. "You've stopped shivering."

I had.

"It's not sexual," he said. I noted he was keeping his tone as emotionless as his expression. "It's clinical."

Clinical. Like a doctor. The last doctor I'd seen had been that homeless drunk Scottie had hired to trail me and then install a tracking device beneath my skin. I wondered what had happened to him when Scottie realized the true bug had gone into a rat's dinner instead.

I caught my lip on my teeth as those memories flooded back and winced because my mouth was split.

Clinical. I didn't want clinical. I wanted outrage. I wanted fury.

I dropped the towel. More than anything, I wanted someone to witness what Scottie's love had done to me. I wanted someone to know how badly that love hurt.

Maddox had seen me in the shower, surely. He'd seen me all but naked as he'd washed me, but still, he sucked in his breath as I squared my shoulders best I could beneath his scrutiny.

"The water cleaned up the nastiness," he said, and his voice was choked up. "So it looks better than it did. How do you feel?" his eyes skirted my breasts and pinned to my nose. I had the feeling it was crooked. It was hard to breathe through.

"Like a stress ball at a banker's convention."

He smiled timidly. "I expected you to say like you'd been hit by Mack Truck." He worked his lip with his teeth, jaw clenched. I noted his hands by his sides were balled into fists.

"I'll be fine," I said, stooping to retrieve the towel.

"Wait," he said.

I peered up at him.

He took a deep breath, bracing, I thought. Something was working its way through him, burrowing like a worm. A struggle was going on behind those eyes.

"May I touch you?"

I stepped away without meaning to and he flushed red in the face.

"Not like that," he said. "I told you. Clinical."

I nodded.

He laid his palm flat on my solar plexus and he inhaled deeply, eyes closed. I was paralyzed as I felt a hum run through his palm and into my tissues. My fingertips buzzed until I felt like I had to shake them out.

And then the most terrifying thing happened.

There was no longer just a hum, but a sound as though a jet engine was taking off between my ears. A thousand pinpricks on my skin came alive.

And it hurt.

A lot.

Molecules and atoms and blood all strained from deep within my tissues toward his palm and each pinprick felt as though some long filament had been yanked on from fathoms of my core and come free all at once.

I might have bowed beneath the onslaught, but Maddox's palm held me aloft. If my feet left the floor I wouldn't have been surprised.

And yet that wasn't the most terrifying thing.

The most terrifying thing came when he finally let me go. He staggered back, gasping for air as though he was too far beneath the waves of a choppy ocean and the pressure was trying to stabilize from too abrupt a resurfacing.

I watched as his head snapped back the way one does when it's struck by a brutal fist. He collapsed to his knees and then to his side, curled into the fetal position. Every discernible part of his body convulsed. It looked for all the world like he was being kicked. Repeatedly.

I stared, dumbstruck and terrified, and felt my feet up-root from the floor only when he sailed across the tiles of my bathroom through the open door and out into the kitchen as though someone had an invisible hand on his collar and was running with him.

I broke free my paralysis right about the same time his name erupted from my lips. I didn't care what exactly was happening or how. I just wanted him to be okay. I rushed along behind him to the kitchen.

I dropped onto the floor, running my hand over his ribs and throat.

I felt for a pulse, not even sure if I would find one in an immortal. Was he immortal? I had no idea. I just kept running over the same things in my mind.

What if he was dying? What if the fae warlord had somehow come back, and finding me still here, was throwing a hissy fit that involved hurting someone I cared about.

Cared about.

It couldn't be possible. I barely knew him.

But he'd helped me. He'd shown compassion when I needed it. And right now, he was convulsing on my kitchen floor.

And it was because of me.

I pressed my palms against his shoulder, thinking I should roll him over to his back, but he swore at me and curled into a tighter ball. I wanted to help. I wanted it to stop.

And I had no idea what to do.

My heart was thudding in my ears with every contortion he made to defend himself from invisible blows. There was something eerily familiar about the way Maddox was reacting.

He wasn't whimpering or crying like I'd done, but he was taking blow for blow by some invisible source and he was feeling each one the way I had.

Somehow, he was reliving Alvin's beating.

My stomach clenched into a hard knot as the realization struck. That had been me. It had been what I'd endured, what I looked like, how I suffered.

I ran to the bathroom.

I barely made it to the bowl before I emptied my stomach of bile and liquid. I was still hanging over the porcelain, watching the swirl of water make a vortex when I heard footsteps at the doorway.

Maddox. Recovered.

I couldn't look at him. I didn't want to.

"Isabella?" he said.

I hung there, too afraid of what I might see, to look up.

"Isabella," he said again. "It's alright, Kitten. It's all alright."

I swallowed another rush of bile and clutched my stomach. I could not look to him. I wouldn't.

"Isabella," he said again. "You don't have to be afraid."

I knew from his tone that he was worried. It seemed unsympathetic to ignore him. I was a lot of things: a thief, a cheat, but I was not a coward.

I peeked sideways at him. Bruises had bloomed on his cheek and his left eye was a bulbous orb that nearly hung over his cheekbone. His lips bloated to twice their size and split in the middle.

It was a flash of an image and no more. I heard my own gasp and then as quickly as I registered the damage, everything smoothed out to normal.

He was the handsome, russet-haired giant again.

Maybe I had imagined it. My body seemed to think it was real. I started to tremble all over and turned so I could sink down onto the toilet.

"It's alright," he murmured. "It's gone. All gone."

"Is it?" I said and planted my forearms across my knees. I didn't think I was going to pass out, but I didn't want to risk it.

"It is," he said.

I heard him take a few hesitant steps and looked up. He crouched in front of me and took one of my hands. He lay the palm against his cheek.

"See? Normal," he said.

I hitched in a few bolstering breaths. Normal. What had just happened was far from normal. Even so, I nodded.

"Normal," I repeated and as though my voice had turned on a switch, I realized I didn't hurt everywhere. Stranger still, I didn't hurt anywhere.

That shouldn't be possible.

He gave me a sad look when I pushed him away and rushed to the sink. I yanked the towel from the mirror.

I looked normal. My hair was wet and I was naked, but there were no blemishes anywhere.

My throat went tight. My fingers clenched the sink because I knew if I didn't hold onto something I was going to collapse. This time for real.

Magic.

Good magic. Magic that felt uplifting and not terrifying.

I could feel my solar plexus trembling. There was always a cost to kindness. Ulterior motives. I'd had to bully my way through protecting my house by blackmailing an outlawed incubus and when I refused to do the fae warlord's bidding, he had taken that earned magic away again.

What would I have to do in return for this gift?

I saw Maddox in the mirror behind me. He looked almost as handsome as ever. He was already smoothing his russet hair back off his face and tucking stray lengths of it behind his ear.

"My God," I said. "What are you?"

CHAPTER 13

I HADN'T MEANT IT to come out like an accusation. I should have shown him gratitude, not fear, but I was too far in its clutches to think straight or give rational reactions. He pursed his lips together.

"What did you do?" I asked. "How?" I wanted to be grateful for whatever it was he'd done, but I was too scared. No one did anything good for nothing.

His shoulders sagged, and he wouldn't meet my eye. Strangely recalcitrant for the arrogant man I knew him to be.

So he did want something. It was as good as an admission.

I pushed away from the sink, disappointed that the near certainty had become certain. I spun around to face him.

"Why?" I asked him, thinking he might answer that one.

He sighed.

"I don't know," he said. And then when I believed he would say more, he stooped to pick up the bath towel and stretched it across my bosom, wrapping it around me and tucking it into itself between my cleavage.

I thought his fingers lingered a little too long between the swell of my breasts, but then he pulled his hand back and tucked it into his trouser pocket.

"You can probably get a decent shower now," he mumbled and then turned to leave the bathroom.

"Wait," I said.

He halted but didn't turn to face me. I watched him place one hand on the door jamb and lean against it. Exhausted, I thought. He was spent.

I could have asked a dozen questions, but I settled on the one that might tick off a few checkboxes.

"Why are you here?" I said.

"I'll tell you when you get dressed," he said. "I'll clean up while you gather your thoughts." He jerked his chin toward the kitchen. I watched him leave and stood for a long moment before I turned on the taps.

The warmth, the soap, the fragrance of the chlorine in the water: all of it felt like luxury. My skin felt fresh and new and as though it had been sheathed in something whose sole purpose was to drink in pleasure and spread it through my core.

I could almost taste the chocolate in the cocoa shampoo.

I made the shower as quick as I could and then skirted through the bathroom and into my bedroom to find my favourite pair of yoga pants and a fuzzy sweatshirt.

Seeing myself in my bedroom mirror, I realized exactly how normal I looked. I hadn't felt normal when I'd woken up. Hadn't felt normal when Maddox found me cringing on the floor.

I looked better than usual. My skin glowed.

Stranger still, I felt distanced from the beating. I would've expected a tremendous amount of PTSD to be swimming around in the mire of memory, but each time my mind touched down on the idea of Alvin in my apartment, the image spread out like smoke when a hand waves through it.

I could still remember each moment, but it had been softened somehow like the touch of fog on bare skin.

I might not have understood why Maddox had done what he had or even exactly what he had done, but I knew that somehow he had taken the violence and the effect of it from me. I'd watched him suffer through it so I could let it go.

I was certain that everything I'd seen happen to him, every bruise and swollen swath of skin, the bulging and sore eye had been exactly what I'd looked like.

And that thought wasn't just discomforting, it was sickening.

I knew only that kindness always had a motive. And this was the most extreme kind of kindness. I couldn't trust it.

I crossed my arms over my chest, desperate almost to stick to the things I knew, not the things that I couldn't explain. I needed something to touch down on, something real and tangible.

There had to be a reason he was here. It wasn't just coincidence that he'd found me at my worst. I needed to know what that was.

I yanked on underwear and my sweats and fluffed out my hair. I grabbed his jacket from its spot on the floor and slung it over my arm. My bug-out bag hunkered under my bed and I grabbed that too.

Time for someone to pay the piper.

I took a deep breath and headed for the kitchen.

Everything was such a confusing muddle that I just couldn't face him straight away. I stopped by at the fridge to pull out a carton of milk. It was half full, and I could barely remember the day I'd bought it, but I upended it without pulling a glass from the cupboard.

It tasted divine. Cold, creamy.

It felt normal.

I could hear him behind me making mock gagging sounds.

"Remind me not to ask you for a glass of milk," he said.

He stood up and stretched, arching his back and reaching out to the sides. He took up a fair bit of space, and while most men would look weary stretching like that, in him it seemed a precursor to something else, the way a boxer warmed up or a musician warmed up his muscles.

"I'm glad to see you're feeling much better," he said.

It almost sounded as though something else was coming. I braced myself. I finished the last of it before turning around to face him and dropped the carton into the trashcan.

"But," I said.

"I need to go."

Going. The word had a ring of finality to it. I wasn't ready for that. I had so many accusations to level. So many questions that needed to be answered. I'd be alone here, for heaven's sake. I didn't even have my cat.

I felt an almost unreasonable sense of panic at the thought of being alone again. It didn't matter that I was fully intending to grab for my bug-out bag and hightail it out of Dodge as soon as I could, I couldn't stand the thought of being alone in my apartment for even that long.

"Oh no," I said. "You're not leaving until you tell me why you came here in the first place."

He quirked one russet eyebrow. "You have literally zero boo-boos and the best question you can come up with is why am I here?" he said and shook his head.

I assumed the gesture was one of disbelief and not disappointment.

"Cheap shot," I said, doing my best to keep my emotional footing. "What did you do to me earlier?"

His shoulders lifted and dropped in a casual shrug. "It was nothing," he said. "I took your pain. My body can hold onto it for you."

"Hold onto it?" I stared at his face, clear of bruises and blood, and remembered how he'd looked just seconds after he'd touched me. I'd not been imagining things. Not at all. "What do you mean?"

He ran a hand over his hair, scrubbing the scalp. "I'm storing it. Temporarily."

I shuttered my eyelids, studying him. "You can do that? For how long?" If it was a temporary thing, I wondered when I could look forward to having all that trauma back.

Something hard lurked behind his gaze, a granite sort of anger. "Until I can find the bastard who did that to you and can give him back every blow he delivered."

He shoved his hands in his trouser pockets as he eyed me, and when his eyes moved from my hands as they tangled over each other at my waist, to my face, I realized he was remembering each bruise. Whatever he saw in my gaze as he caught it, must have bothered him because he crossed the room to stand in front of me.

Watching him move put me in mind of the old cliché of watching a big cat on the prowl. In comparison to Alvin's cement blockhouse stature, Maddox's was languid, but it was just as dangerous.

He loomed over me for a long moment, looking down into my face. I thought his gaze landed like a moth on my mouth but then he lifted his suit jacket from over the crook in my elbow and dug his fingers into the pocket and the moment was gone.

I bit down on my lip without meaning to as his fingers came out of his pocket holding a cell phone.

"Silly me," he said. "In all of the hubbub at the museum, I forgot to take my cell phone out of the pocket before I rescued a damsel in distress."

He ran the back of his hand down my hair. "Take care, Kitten," he said and spun on his heel.

"I wasn't in distress," I said sullenly to his back.

He paused with his hand on the doorknob. "Damsels never are," he said in an indulgent tone.

Encouraged, I scanned the room quickly for a pair of shoes.

"Let me follow along for a little bit."

"Oh, Kitten," he said, over his shoulder. "Where I'm going, you don't want to follow."

CHAPTER 14

"You still didn't tell me how you found my apartment?" I said, emboldened.

"My phone's geo locater information led me here."

I noted he said nothing about the way he found me. Nothing about how I'd ended up that way. I would have thought he'd be interested. Especially after what he'd experienced. No word about what he thought might happen to me if the person who had done that to me came around again. No question about why I wanted to follow him to God knew where.

I glanced at the front door. The cars in the streets were already rolling by, pedestrians heading out for brunch or family's houses for Sunday lunch. Scottie would be out less than twelve hours now.

He twisted the knob. In seconds he'd be gone, and I didn't even have a shoe on.

"I know what you were after at the gala," I said.

"Who said I was there to steal anything?" he said and pulled the door open. The sound of a cab horn blared in at me.

I pushed the door closed and leaned against it, staring up at him.

"I'm not a thief. Merely a broker," he said.

"You were after something, same as Scottie was," I said, ignoring the way his body language told me what he thought of thieves. "Scottie and you and your hoodlums were there for a reason."

He grinned, easing my anxiety some.

"I've never heard Kerri called a hoodlum before," he said, "But do enlighten me. Who is this Scottie person and why would I be after the same thing he is?"

I chewed my lip, trying to decide if he was toying with me. "Scottie was the burly guy with the gun."

"Ah, yes. Your beau."

"Not my beau. The man who..." I couldn't hold his eye as I thought about what had happened to me because of Scottie. I struggled to explain why it mattered to me that they were both at the museum and both involved somehow with my lesson.

"So?" I said because I knew I'd already lost that fight. "What was it?"

He sighed indulgently, if not a bit resigned, and then he slipped his fingers into his jacket pocket and pulled out a coin.

I grabbed it from his fingers.

"You used me to steal that," I said.

I wasn't sure whether I was more incensed that he'd pretended not to be a thief or that it had been on me the whole time and I'd not known.

I glared at him and the coin alternately. It was real. It had heft and it had a rough texture from being pocked with age.

"Not steal," he said. "You don't steal something that's yours. We were on a recovery mission, not a robbery." There was a specific inflection to his tone that made me think he was offended. "And it's not a coin. It's a stone."

I glared at him, not the least bit mollified by his seeming umbrage. I doubted the coin was his, but I wasn't about to argue. I was the one who had been put at risk, after all. And I had the distinct impression that I'd been a happy happenstance that they'd exploited under the ruse of rescuing me.

I ignored the fact that I would've done the same, after all.

"And If I'd gotten caught with this in your pocket? What if they traced it here? To me?"

"Easy, Kitten," he said. "No one's coming looking for it. You're safe."

"No?" I demanded.

"No," he said. "There's a pretty good fake slipped into the curator's pocket. I imagine he's having a devil of a time explaining things to the police right about now."

"Now," he said. "I do have to go."

Apparently, he wasn't going to wait, and I wasn't going to stay there.

I grabbed a pair of sneakers from the landing and followed him out the door. I pulled it shut behind me, hopscotching across the stoop as I yanked the running shoes over each heel.

I followed him down my steps and into the street. It was raining, a cold, driving sort of precipitation that clawed its way beneath my collar.

I dug my cell phone from my bag, keeping it covered by my palm from the weather. I was surprised to see the screen show it was past 6 pm. Where had the day gone? I needed all the hours I had at my disposal.

I had to make three strides for every one of Maddox's, and I even then it was a flat-out jog to keep up once I did fall into step with him. Wherever he was going, it was in a hurry. The raindrops had created a rivulet down his nape. One long hank of russet hair curled around his jawline toward the front of his chin.

"Where are we going?" I asked stepping up my pace even more as he did.

"Our separate ways," he said, without slowing down.

I felt as though the further I got away from my apartment the better chance I had of escaping Scottie's clutches altogether.

"The hell we are," I said. "You don't understand. I just need an escort for a short while. I'm not safe here anymore. Scottie will be back, eventually--he might even be somewhere lurking around right now. And with the glamor gone, he'll get in the same way you did, and I'll be a sitting duck."

He stopped in the middle of the sidewalk. "Glamor?"

I paused to look at him. Surely he'd heard of glamor if I had heard of it.

"Yes. Some fae warlord said my apartment was in his realm."

I waved my hand in front of my face to dissuade him from asking questions. "Don't ask. It has something to do with a nasty incubus and buying me a favour. But as it turns out, this Fae warlord thinks I owe him."

"They do like to be repaid," he said thoughtfully.

I clutched my hands to my chest in an effort to keep them from wrestling each other. "So I've discovered."

"He called himself a fae warlord?"

"He called himself *she* at one point. I suppose a fae could be gender-fluid." I shrugged, not really caring how the fae self-identified in light of the pickle I was in.

He chuckled, which surprised me.

"What?" I demanded.

"Sidhe," he said, spelling out the word. "Some might say a sidhe is a breed of fae. A very old breed. And many of them wouldn't use the term fae to describe themselves." He put his finger to his lips, thoughtful. "If a sidhe warlord came to you and wants--what was it he wanted--?"

"A bone of some sort," I said with a sigh. "But it doesn't matter. I'm already screwed. The glamor's gone, as you can see. Then you show up out of nowhere to pick up a priceless artifact I had no idea I was stowing for you--one that could have gotten me arrested, mind you--"

"You weren't," he said shortly.

"But I could have been," I argued. "I could have gone to jail." I thought of Scottie again and imagined the way he'd be prowling about the general cells, waiting to be released if he wasn't already, and that brought me right straight back to Alvin. I stepped up my pace once more.

"And then you make some weird mojo on me," I said. "What was that anyway?" I said, clutching at his sleeve so I could hold him still long enough to get ahead of him.

He didn't stop but it gave me the chance to scuffle ahead of him and turn my back to the oncoming traffic, so I could see his face. "What was that?"

He halted and shrugged. "Mojo," he said.

"Not a great answer."

"Not a great question."

"You aren't going to tell me, are you?"

He said nothing. That inscrutable facade remained intact. I heaved a sigh, beaten for the moment.

"Then at least tell me where we're going," I said.

"If you insist on coming, then you'll see, won't you?"

He stuck out his hand and a cab pulled alongside the curb. Maddox handed him a fifty and bade him take us to the seedier part of town, or as the locals called it, Paradise.

We jumped out in front of Paradise's old library, the one I'd met Kassie in a few weeks earlier when I'd been running from Finn, and I looked askance at him.

"Feeling the need for a bodice ripper?" I asked him.

"You're a better comedian than you are a thief," he said.

"I'm not--"

He held up his hand. "Save it."

He lifted his nose to the air as though scenting for something. I swallowed down a wisecrack about dogs.

After a moment, he made a short grunting sound that could have meant, *figures*, and then he turned down a side street.

"Keep up," he said. "I don't want to have to have to start looking for you too if someone decides you'd make a nice quick meal."

"I've been down this way before," I said haughtily from his side.

He paused long enough to look me over and made a thoughtful sound deep in his throat.

"What?" I said. "I do business all over. No one has touched me before. They might even like me down here." That one was a stretch, but I didn't like the implication in his tone that I was a helpless twit.

Instead of arguing he started walking again. In three strides he had managed to make me take to running. I had short legs and though I was a good runner, running in an area like this usually meant it was from something, and under the circumstances, it might not be a good idea.

"Mind slowing down a bit, then?" I said.

He sighed and held back. "We don't have much time," he said and reached back for my hand. He gripped it tightly and squeezed.

I flushed at his touch.

"Keep up or I'll drag you," he said and the warm flush evaporated.

"Bastard," I muttered, but I kept up, if only to spite him. It wasn't long before we arrived at a seedy bar much like the Rot Gut Tavern and a mere couple of blocks away.

The exterior had bullet holes in the paint and graffiti that someone had graffitied over. As scary as Fayed's bar could be, this one seemed just downright nefarious.

"If you need a drink, Fayed's would be less filthy," I said as we stood outside, surveying the door and the numerous wounds it had endured in its time.

"I didn't come for a drink," he said.

He prodded my chest with a finger, pushing me back gently but firmly.

He held me off that way while he gazed down at me. His eyes pinned to my mouth for a long moment, making me uncomfortable.

"You should stay outside," he finally said.

I mentally ran down a list of reasons why he wouldn't want me to follow him and one in particular rattled its way to the top. He had a priceless coin. A coin he'd used me to steal.

"I want half," I said quickly. "Fifty percent off the top."

At first, he looked confused and then as realization lit his face, he guffawed.

"You want half of what's waiting in there?" he said.

I nodded.

He shook his head. "You're not a kitten; you're a bull."

"Forty, then."

He shook his head. "You don't want a tenth of what's waiting inside, Isabella."

He gave me a shove, but I kept my footing even if it took considerable effort to do so.

I lifted my chin as though I was going to argue and waited till he cocked that russet eyebrow in warning.

I conceded. Just the right amount of time, I thought, and watched him push open the door and disappear into the gloom within.

I gave him exactly four seconds before I followed him in.

I quietly scooted along the wall to the right as he strode immediately toward the bar. He was so intent, I doubted he knew I was there behind him, but I could imagine the scowl that creased his face from the set of his shoulders, the way his muscles moved like a cat's beneath it.

He was flexing his fists at his sides as he headed to the bar, curling and uncurling them. He was nervous. Anxious. Eager. All things that would match up with an uncertain sale of priceless items.

But there was something else that I recognized from the many times I'd watched the same emotions in Scottie's body language.

He was furious.

He'd hidden it well from me but now that he thought I was safely outside, he gave it free rein.

Even the half dozen patrons could see it. Several of them got up from the bar and, pulling their beers along with them, shuffled casually toward the pool tables. All but one of them, and that man hung over the counter oblivious to the way the others turned their backs on him almost intentionally.

They saw what I saw and reacted the way strangers do. They decided to ignore it.

Maddox approached that beefy man hanging over the bar. Even from this distance, I could see the swelling on the back of the man's hand as he reached for his drink. He stretched his fingers wide, showing several bloody cracks in the knuckles. Knuckles that had buried themselves into my cheeks and ribs just hours earlier.

Alvin. The bastard.

My stomach knotted up at sight of him, and the strength ran out my legs like water from a tap. I found the nearest chair and sank into it, aware that my breathing had gotten too loud, too short.

I sucked it in and held it, trying to reset it as Maddox approached him and Alvin turned at the sound of someone approaching him. Maybe he felt the fury or the tension. Maybe he felt the shift in the room.

Confusion twisted his features at first as he spun on his stool to face Maddox, but then they contorted in annoyance.

"Fuck you want?" he said, a little too loudly.

Maddox said nothing. Nothing. As long as I lived, I would never forget the sound of that silence.

He just reached out toward Alvin and spidered his fingers across the man's face. I'd thought Alvin a bloated and unfit man until he'd beaten me, mistaken the size of him for fat.

The truth was, he was big, as big and as muscle-hardened as any thug Scottie had employed, but he was nowhere near as big as Maddox. Side by side, it was obvious who was the giant and who was Jack.

Maddox's fingers went into Alvin's hairline even as his palm all but covered Alvin's face.

And then the bastard rose from his stool. Rose. As though being lifted or levitating but I knew neither of those could be true. A man can't be lifted by his face, and a man can't levitate. Yet Alvin's feet dangled and kicked at Maddox as he was lifted toward the tar-stained ceiling.

I'd mistaken also the length of Maddox's arms until one stretched upward, holding Alvin by his face. Alvin mumbled and tried to shout for help beneath his palm.

Everyone in the bar swelled forward in surprise and interest. They smelled blood.

Even the bartender leaned forward, his hand reaching beneath the bar.

I expected a gun or a bat to come out but in the next heartbeat, Alvin began to convulse beneath Maddox's hand. The sheer violence of it paralyzed the bartender, paralyzed me and the half dozen other patrons.

He twisted and curled his knees up, grunted in pain.

Bruises and blood bloomed on his face and neck. Instead of gripping Maddox by the arm to defend himself, he winced and hugged himself. Bones cracked, loud snapping sounds echoed in the room, punctuated by muffled screams.

The invisible beating continued, and though I couldn't hear punches and kicks being landed, I could hear the resulting strikes resonating from Alvin's body.

Prickles of cold swept across my skin and water flooded my mouth. My stomach rebelled.

I couldn't get to my feet fast enough to run to the bathroom. I had to heave beneath the table. The stink of sour bile washed over me, and my belly trembled from the effort of trying to calm itself.

As terrified as I was, as gut sick over what was happening, I made the mistake of looking up and catching Maddox's eye.

The timing couldn't have been more wrong. I thought I smelled excrement and urine. Alvin. He'd released his bowel and bladder and he now hung, slumped into himself from Maddox's grip.

With one short movement, Maddox released him, and the man who had beaten me to within an inch of paralysis fell to the floor in a heap.

The patrons sped for the exits.

Maddox's face, his expression, was unrecognizable in its vengeful fury, and in those seconds, terror overran the sickness. "You killed him," I said, gagging on the words.

CHAPTER 15

I WASN'T SURE WHAT to expect. Maybe I expected to feel vindicated or relieved. Maybe even a sense of peace. I felt none of those things.

Alvin might have been the fists that pummelled me, the feet that kicked me, but he was the weapon only. Alvin was a tool like a hammer was a tool.

The real person wielding the weapon was Scottie, and Alvin was nothing if not a loyal weapon. Scottie owned him. Owned his life. Just like any other person circling within Scottie's orbit, if that life was to be snuffed out, it would be at Scottie's behest, not anyone else's.

And there would always be more Alvins. Except next time, that Alvin would be a bigger weapon, wielded by an angrier owner.

"He's dead," I said again and the way my voice sounded accusing rather than aghast, I knew I was only just beginning to add up the fact that this was Maddox, the man standing in front of me, who had done it.

"You killed him," I said.

Maddox looked down at the husk of man in a heap at his feet.

"Apparently," he said.

He sounded almost as though he hadn't expected Alvin to die. I had a hard time swallowing every time I glanced at the bloody rags and hulking figure curled into a ball at Maddox's feet. My gorge kept rising and my skin was prickling with flush. I thought I could feel my nails biting into my palms.

"You think that will fix anything?" I said, a little too shrilly. "It fixes nothing."

I staggered to my feet, aiming for the door.

Maddox's gaze landed on mine and held it. My feet rooted themselves to the floor.

"This isn't the bastard that did that to you?"

My head jangled up and down. "Of course it is."

I felt myself backing away from Maddox the way the bartender had.

"It is, yes. It's him, but he's just the messenger. There will be more. There's always more. You didn't fix anything. You made it worse."

Maddox's gaze shuttered dangerously. "The man at the gala?" he said, so low I barely heard him, and it was the threat of it that reached my ears more than the level. "He is the author of this particularly nasty note?"

He nudged Alvin with his toe as though he was killing time until I answered, but I knew he didn't need me to. He had every piece of info he needed.

And so, it seemed, did the bartender, who finally made the decision to reach for his phone.

Maddox gave him a long look and the man dropped it onto the counter. He put up his hands. The screen died to black.

"Didn't see nothing," the bartender said. "I'll say nothing. No one will know. Just leave."

Maddox's fists clenched and unclenched at his sides. The bartender sidled sideways like a snake trying to get out of the reach of a stick. He butted up against edge of his counter.

"Seriously," he said. "I don't even know how it happened. Bunch of thugs, is all," he said, weaving out a plausible tale as best he could with Maddox staring him down. "Bunch of thugs dropped him in here."

He grabbed the glass Alvin had been drinking from and emptied it out in the sink. Washed it clean. Put it back on the shelf. "See?" he said. "Didn't even have a drink in here."

I felt myself begin to hyperventilate. Kassie and Fayed had both told me Maddox was dangerous. And it wasn't as though I didn't believe them. I just didn't have an opportunity to see exactly what form that danger came in.

I flicked my gaze over his shoulder toward the bartender who was backing away from the bar, his gaze pinned to Maddox's back.

"No," Maddox said and crouched down next to Alvin. "No need to make up a story," he said.

The bartender sighed heavily. Relief spread across his shoulders.

Maddox glanced up at me, ignoring the bartender for the moment. "Where should I dump him?"

I was struggling to keep up, struggling to stay calm.

"Dump him?" I said. I felt as though everything was speeding up and slowing down all at once.

"Yes, Isabella," Maddox said, impatience a barely concealed tone in a voice that held me like a terrified child. "Where should I return this message back to its author?"

Back to Scottie. He wanted to dump Alvin at Scottie's doorstep. I felt my shoulders heaving, my stomach threatened to rebel again. I heard the echoes of my memory telling me I might care about this man, a man I thought might have some compassion inside.

But he was just like Scottie.

Maybe they were all like Scottie. Maybe I was better off alone. I couldn't go home. I had no way of getting out of the city. I shook my bug-out bag, testing its weight. The last time I'd dug into it, had been to take the cache out to pay for the museum intel. My escape funds were all but gone.

I sobbed out loud and caught it between my teeth.

"Isabella," Maddox said, and it was his voice that freed me from my own paralysis finally.

I ran headlong toward the door.

Maddox sighed from behind me as though this was the last thing he needed. He called out to me again, but it was too late now for me to even turn around. I was at the door and the handle was in my hand and I was tearing out of there like a cat with its tail on fire.

Cat. My cat. Trapped in my apartment in the fae's realm. Strange how that was the thought that struck me as I fled the bar.

Strange it was the thing to remind me.

I really was alone.

It was dark already, and the street was filling up with hookers and thieves. My people. People I understood. Normal, human, mortal people.

I caught my breath and leaned against a wall, heaving. My shoulders dug into the bricks. All I could think of was the way Alvin had twisted in Maddox's grip, suffering blows and kicks he couldn't see coming.

He suffered, oh how he suffered. My body had echoed each moment of the attack and though I hadn't felt a bit of pain, the cells remembered it and cried out to my mind.

I hated Alvin for what he'd done to me. I hated Scottie for ordering it.

But while I might not have been inclined to feel pity for Alvin, my psyche ached beneath each assault, the memory of it making me sick to my stomach even if I felt nothing.

And worse was that it had been Maddox who delivered that beating. I squeezed my eyes shut, not wanting to put those pieces of the puzzle together.

"I told you to stay outside," came a soft whisper. "I warned you not to come in with me."

Maddox. Trying to backtrack and blame me for feeling this way. It was too much, that accusation, as though I was some-how to blame for witnessing something I shouldn't have. As though he wasn't culpable at all. I needed to get away from him. From here. I needed a safe space.

But nowhere was safe. I knew that now. Not my apartment. Not with Maddox.

I pushed off the building. He caught my arm momentarily and tugged me toward him, but I fought him like a cat would fight. I hissed out curses at him, kicking, scratching.

"Leave me alone," I said, striking out. I connected with something. Maybe his cheekbone. I wasn't sure. I was so blind-ed by confusion and anger and fear that I couldn't know where the blows landed.

"Isabella."

My name was a command in the air. Stay put, it said. Stop.

I would do nothing of the sort.

"Fuck you," I said and made one last bid for escape. This time, one of my kicks landed against something solid. He grunted and let go.

I fled out of instinct, aiming for the shadows.

I didn't think. I didn't rationalize. I just let that instinct take me wherever it would. I didn't stop running long enough to catch my breath or check to see if Maddox followed me.

My feet knew the streets, my night vision knew the alley-ways, the trashcans, even the rats that skittered along the walls of the buildings. Familiar smells of garlic and onions and the occasional waft of toast and cigarette smoke wrapped around me like a shawl. I felt safer in that darkness with each step.

I would have been surprised to find myself anywhere but Fayed's bar.

By the time I saw its neon sign above the door, and the distinct smell of urine and blood prickled its way up my nose as I crossed the threshold, I was winded and exhausted. Far more than spent.

The adrenaline that had soaked my tissues when Alvin died and then propelled me along the streets finally wasted and fizzled out.

The result was a complete collapse into the first chair I saw upon entering. Without looking to see who was in the room, I dropped my head onto my arms and let go a monsoon of tears onto the table.

Judging by the way chairs scraped the floor and the patrons mumbled in confusion, I guessed the men were pretty uncom-fortable witnessing a human woman's misery.

I laughed into my arms at my own description of the patrons being men. What a hoot. I knew now these were not men. I'd discovered just how inhuman they were once Finn had set me to his impossible task. My blinders were no longer on. I knew every single man in this place was an otherworld creature of some sort. Witches, warlocks, Yetis. Who knew what.

I only knew I was a human in a room full of things that weren't. For all I knew the bar was filled with blood-sucking vampires.

"Isabella?"

The voice was soft and thickly accented. Fayed. I knew it without even looking up.

"This is the only place I'm safe," I said, mumbling into my shirt sleeve.

A chair scraped the floor and I felt him settle beside me. He smelled of fragrant spices and copper wire.

"This is the first time I've heard of a bleeder bar being safe for a human woman," he said, and his palm settled between my shoulder blades.

I lay my cheek on my arms as I looked at him. "Bleeder bar?" I said. "This is the first time I've heard it called that."

His thin smile disappeared as he shrugged. "Humans pay attention to the alcohol in the bottles; creatures of the night pay attention to the humans seeing the booze. You're human," he said. "Do you think we would advertise this place that way for the beings who are not?"

A furtive survey of the land showed me three wiry men clustered around a standing bar at the back. Fayed was watching them intently in between stealing glances at me.

I sighed. "Why tell me now?"

"After what we went through together here, what's the point in hiding it from you?"

He was talking about the way Kelly the assassin had hunted me down and nearly killed me here.

"You saved me then."

He leaned back in his chair, propping his boots up onto the table next to me.

"Oh yes," he said. "That I did. More times than you know. It's why you shouldn't have come back."

"Maddox is a murderer," I blurted out and while I might have expected Fayed to protest or look surprised, he just pulled his boots back off the table and leaned close, brushing my hair from my temples.

"Many of us are," he said as he peered into my eyes.

I felt slightly woozy looking into them. I planted both palms on the table and sat up straight, trying to gather my thoughts into a skein that I could thread to a palpable knot of conclusion. One that articulated exactly what was bothering me when I had run to a vampire for help.

"I just saw him kill a man."

His eyebrow cocked ever so slightly but he said nothing. Instead, he flicked his wrist toward the cluster of men who snarled and prowled their way to the pool table, well out of earshot, I hoped.

"And you chose to come here, where you know the place will be filled with other preternatural creatures who will kill before the night is out."

"I feel safe here."

"You shouldn't."

CHAPTER 16

My throat grew tight. How many times had I drank here, quietly assuming it was no more dangerous than Scottie's seedy bars.

"I am safe here," I squeaked out, insistent. I had to be. I had nothing else.

"This place is not safe for mundanes," he said and squeezed my hand. "In fact, this whole quarter is more supernatural than mundane. Those who find their way here often don't find their way home again."

Someone placed a glass of water down beside my hand on the table, a youngish woman. She was mid-height, which meant she would be taller than me if I stood next to her. Brunette.

She held a pitcher of water in one hand and something about the way she did it looked familiar.

"Thanks," I said, catching her eye. "Have we met?"

I scanned through my memory to find a match.

She glanced briefly at Fayed as though requesting permission to speak and yet there was something behind that expression that bespoke cunningness and not demureness. I wondered if Fayed saw it.

Fayed cleared his throat. "Ismé," he said. "Isabella, Ismé is our new server."

My glance fleeted unwittingly to her wrist. I should have remembered the face, but it was the bruises on her skin that did it. I knew right then who she was: the server from the gala, the one I was supposed to meet for drinks. I noted that two more 'cat bites' had bloomed on her arm.

"We have met," I said, remembering where I'd seen her before. "The museum gala. You were serving."

I made my best effort to scan past the bite marks on her wrist because now that I knew she'd got them from feeding a vampire, I also connected just who the vampire was.

I wasn't sure I liked knowing that.

"You were the champagne lady," I said to cover up the way I couldn't look at her all of a sudden.

I reached for the glass and noticed my fingers trembled. So. No less panicked than when I'd arrived despite having a good view of the door and a companionable ear. I hated that I had to clutch the glass to keep my hand from shaking.

She gave me a narrowed eye outlined in far too much eyeliner.

"I was there, yes," she said. "But we didn't meet."

Then I realized she wouldn't know me. I'd been dressed as Ginger, the hot chick with the rose tattoo.

And I'd stood her up.

"Ouch," I said with a pitiful chuckle. As cover ups went, it wasn't my best, but I figured there was less harm in seeming to be an unnoticed and unremembered plain Jane than give away my alias from the night before.

"Don't worry, hun," she said. "There's a lot I don't remember from that night. Things went to shit pretty quick back there if you know what I mean." She shook her head as though she were remembering it.

I nodded. I did. It was a hell of a night. A hell of a morning. And I didn't want to go there again because that memory led me straight to Maddox.

I turned Fayed's hand upside down on the table and laid mine against his palm. "You have to let me stay here," I said. "Just for a couple of days. I don't have anywhere else to go."

I stared him straight in the eye. "I've gotten mixed up in something over my head and I can't go home."

I squeezed my eyes shut, trying to keep the panic at saying the words aloud suppressed.

"Isabella," he sighed. "I can't keep my clients away from you forever. Sooner or later, one of them is going to challenge me for you. And some of them are older than I am. Some aren't even vampires. You're going to have to figure it out."

"That's just it," I muttered. "There's nothing to figure out. There's no puzzle to solve. I'm just stuck between a rock and a rock."

I'd lost the safety of my apartment. I'd spent all my bug-out cash on a lead that ended up taking me nowhere. I'd lost the chance to keep the glamor that kept me safe.

If I even wanted to help the sidhe warlord now, even if I begged, how would he hear? It's not like I could call him up with my cell phone. I had my bug-out bag. There was an alias ID in there. I could leave the city. Scottie might not even think to look for an alias until it was too late and even then, he might not have intel on the name I used.

He'd find me of course; I'd be fooling myself if I thought he'd ever give up looking, but it would take him months. Maybe years. Heck, Alvin might not have even passed on my address to Scottie before Maddox...

"Well, before Maddox took care of that loose end."

"Maddox? What did he do?"

I stared at Fayed. Apparently, that last I'd said out loud. I took a drink of water; it was icy and it felt good going down, almost like putting out a hot fire in my throat. Fayed said no more, just watched me. Judging by the way his face softened, I must be looking better by the minute. Less frantic.

He laid his hand on mine when I put the glass back down. I expected his touch to be cold, but it was searing the way ice can be if left on your skin too long. I ran my gaze along his forearm to his face.

He caught my eyes with his and held them. When he spoke, a pin dropping in the room would have been louder than his voice, and yet I could hear each word as though they were my own thoughts.

"What does this someone want from you that you would run here to a blood bar instead of your own home?" His gaze narrowed, and I thought behind those gorgeous lashes the eyes had turned blood red. "What did Maddox do to you?"

"Not Maddox," I said. "Not really." I wasn't sure why I was defending a murderer, except that the murderer had relieved me of some pretty horrible physical pain. He didn't deserve for me to imply he'd done me harm when he hadn't.

"Who, then?" That heavy weight of his gaze again, seeing beyond my eyes to the back of my skull. "What's going on?"

I felt compelled to explain everything, but the long habit of secrecy instilled by fists and barbed words kept my tongue silent. I had to weigh the consequences, figure out if things could get worse or better.

He waited patiently, as though he fully expected me to answer and it was that expectation that did it. I told him everything I knew, everything that had happened.

Talking it out helped some. It helped me see I had few choices anyway, the way I saw it. Two, to be exact.

"I can either help the fae warlord and get my glamor back, or I can leave the city," I said.

"Helping any fae is not a good idea."

"Leave the city it is, then," I said and pushed myself to my feet. "I've already seen what owing the fae means." I looked down at him. "Pinning my hopes on magic to help me was my first mistake. I won't make it again."

He smiled but it didn't reach his eyes. "Be sure you don't," he said. "Fae magic can't be trusted."

"You sound like you speak from experience."

He got to his feet, too, and laid his hand on my shoulder. The way he looked down at me, I knew he understood the sense of hopelessness and wanted to at least make me feel less alone.

"There's always a cost you don't expect, Isabella. One that's hidden within the request. They ask things in riddles so it can be twisted and tainted to their own ends. More bang for their magical buck."

"Got it," I said. "Do not help the fae find his bone." I laughed out loud at the words. They sounded sexual, and the thought that I could laugh meant I was beginning to feel as though a crucial decision had made its way through my psyche.

I leaned over to plant a kiss on Fayed's cheek. I did feel a thousand pounds lighter. I felt as though I could put it all behind me: Scottie, the fae warlord, Maddox.

I clicked my heels together the way Dorothy did at her own decision. It wasn't as though I could pretend a supernatural realm didn't exist; I'd never be able to forget that, but I could at least start over. Out of Scottie's reach. And without that threat, I wouldn't need the fae or Maddox.

I should have left weeks ago.

"I'm glad my feet brought me here." I smiled for him, so he'd know just how glad I was. Especially since I wouldn't see him again.

"Think nothing of it," he said and tapped his fingers on the table top. He looked uncomfortable, awkward. It was best I just leave now, and I tilted an imaginary hat before spinning on my heel.

"Isabella?" he said, catching my wrist.

I halted and faced him, expectant.

He heaved a sigh that shuddered all the way down to his shoulders, then he went to the bar and hit a button on the cash register. He pulled out a wad of cash and when he came back, he stuffed it into my hand.

I knew what he was doing, and I felt a rush of gratitude that he would fund my departure this way.

"I'll pay you back," I said.

His mouth twitched, and he shook his head.

"Don't take this the wrong way," he said. "But don't come back."

I glanced at the men in the corner and saw they were watching us intently. I shivered without meaning to.

"Don't worry," I said. "I'm good as gone. Colin will have to fetch his own bone from a bunch of vampires. I won't be his towel-girl."

"Seethe," he said, correcting me. "A bunch of vampires is called a seethe."

"Got that too," I said. "Not that it will matter if I'm lucky."

"Vampires exist right here, Isabella. We don't travel world to world like the fae or the gods. We used to be human. Our energies exist here with our bodies. It's our souls that are in a different realm."

"So you have souls?"

"Used to," he said. "And I feel its loss like a phantom limb. Many of us do."

He leaned against the bar.

"Sometimes the best of us find a way to use that specter soul as a sort of replacement. Most of us don't. But make no mistake: we are everywhere."

As I strode to the door, I could hear him behind me rattling glasses. I didn't need to turn around to know he was back at the bar.

I was out into the cool night air before I realized I'd left my bug-out bag on the table and I turned with a grin toward the door, a joke about being gone too long on my tongue.

But some movement caught my eye and I paused, trying to see out into the alley past the garbage bins and shadowy trees.

The girl from the museum crouched in the middle of the alley, looking for all the world like she was handwashing a bit of laundry in a dirty puddle left over from the rain.

I wasn't sure if it was the neon lights, but the water didn't look right. It had a cast to it, a reddish glint where the light hit it. And the garment she was rinsing looked familiar. It was silky and khaki green.

The dress I'd worn to the museum, I realized, and even as my mind cast about for the explanation why she would have my dress and how she might have gotten it, she stood in front of me.

She pulled the dress along with her and it snaked down her side like coils of entrails.

That's when I noticed she was naked.

And covered in blood.

CHAPTER 17

My first reaction was a protective one. Whatever she was doing standing there in the middle of the alleyway, naked and covered in blood, would come second to making sure she wasn't fatally hurt.

I had no idea what to do for her. Even if she wasn't in mortal danger, she had to be traumatized and rushing her would no doubt send whatever vestiges of sanity she clung to running for the exits.

Whatever had done that to her couldn't have made it an easy go.

I called over my shoulder to Fayed and then regretted it. I was too shrill. It would scare her.

My stomach was in knots at the way she looked. Maybe it was already too late.

I took my time advancing on her and she held her ground like a deer about to bolt. I splashed through the puddle and a spray of water shot up beneath my T-shirt and soaked my clothes. It seeped in over my shoes. I didn't expect it to be so cold.

If it was that cold on my feet, shod in sneakers, no doubt she was freezing. How long had she been out there? Had one of the vampires from inside accosted her?

I held my hands out toward her, reaching in a way I hoped wasn't threatening. The last thing I wanted to do was spook her.

"It's okay, honey," I said, keeping my voice low and calm. "It's okay. You're safe now."

I had no idea if that was true, but it could be. And it certainly seemed the right thing to say.

"Are you a vampire?" she said.

"No," I said. "Nothing like that. I just want to help you."

She twisted her head so that it faced the door to the bar and yet still somehow managed to show me full view of a face lacking any expression. Deadpan. That's what it was. She was in shock. If she wasn't so obviously hurt, I'd be creeped out by that look.

I was only a few feet away, so close to touching her, but not close enough. I tried to see past all the blood to find wounds or bruises, cuts or bite marks. My mind was already reeling with what I'd have to do if she had some unseen gusher somewhere.

I tried to flicker back to my First Aid training and came up with nothing but CPR instructions. Where in the hell was Fayed?

Her gaze flicked from the door back to me. "Not a vampire," she said. "But a friend of vampires."

Whatever knots had twisted through my stomach were nothing to the sound of accusation in her voice.

"I'm no friend of anything that would hurt a young girl."

Incredibly, she took a step toward me. A rush of hope made me gasp. I nodded at her stupidly.

"That's it," I said. "I want to help."

One more step. This time much steadier. I felt my heart slow down.

"That's right, honey," I said. "I can help."

I took another step through the water and this time it got me close enough that I could touch her with my fingers if I reached out. I swallowed. Nervous.

She held out the bloody dress to me and I plucked it from her grasp with a rush of relief. The worst was over. She was going to let me close. Let me help.

The cloth was cold and wet and still slimy in my grip, and all I could think to do with it was to toss it at the nearest dumpster. It landed a few feet away, coiling into a thing that looked like wet viscera.

With careful, quiet movements, I pulled off my coat and held it out to her with one hand. I waited to see if she'd run, faint, or collapse.

She did none of them. Buoyed, I leaned close so I could wrap it over her shoulders, pulled it tightly together. I had the presence of mind to run my hand along her throat and wrists, checking for wounds or gaping cuts or something that would account for the amount of blood.

But even as my fingers touched her skin, I realized that the blood was nothing but a trick of the light. There was no fluid on her skin. It was dry and unblemished and soft like the fuzz of the newborn's. Perhaps too soft, the way the foam of dish-water feels as you plunge your hand in beneath the bubbles.

But that didn't make sense.

"You're a strange one," she said, looking up at me. "No wonder Morrigan enjoys you so much."

Something was off. Something I couldn't put my finger on. Those eyes were too mature for her age. They sparked within like a blade slicing across a beam of light.

I took an involuntary step backward, letting go the material. The jacket gaped open again, showing a delicate collarbone.

No blood at all. Clean, unblemished skin. I could barely lift my eyes from the way the bones curved and moved as she did.

"You're not human," I said.

She grinned, flashing perfectly even teeth that looked like they might have been filed into small points.

"Where is she?" the girl said.

More water seeped into my shoes as I scuffed backwards. She advanced for each step I took.

"Tell us where she is, and we'll intervene," she said.

"Intervene in what?" I was scared now.

She glanced at the coil of dress, still showing bloody and torn beside the dumpster.

"Your death."

My death. Those words coming from the mouth of a teenager were chilling enough, but the way it sounded on her lips, expectant, premonitory. Every muscle went tense. I felt as though the blackness swimming at the edges of my eyesight had darkened my hearing too. I couldn't feel my feet.

"Who are you?" I managed to get out. I wiggled my toes, trying to get some sense of feeling back, enough that I could scuffle backwards. I needed to back up because she was coming at me, slowly, with measured steps, but advancing. My chest shuddered.

I could swear she was getting taller with each step. The eyes that looked too mature began to match the features.

"You're afraid," she said, but it wasn't surprise in her voice or empathy.

There was no tone at all in it in fact; and all I could think was she was dead. She was a ghost or a spirit and she had no humanity or emotion in her.

"Stay away from me," I said, reaching backward to see how close I was to the door.

"Don't be afraid," she said. "Death comes for all."

She spread her arms wide as though to embrace me. "Warriors must be ready to face it."

"I'm no warrior," I protested. "Just a regular mortal with a need to get out of the city. Let me pass."

She took another step. "I don't bar your way."

I looked past her but found I couldn't bring myself to sprint by. She watched me thinking it through.

I was out of the puddle; my shoes were catching on dry asphalt. I stumbled and caught myself before I could fall.

"What are you?" I said.

She chuckled, a low and throaty sound that didn't have a hint of sanity in it. She was mad, I thought. Totally gone.

"I was trying to help you," I protested, knowing it probably didn't matter to her, but for some reason it mattered to me.

It seemed incredibly important and that the tables being turned was unfair somehow. Foul play. The worst of repayments for a good deed.

I was just a few feet away from the bar's door. A rat squealed from the dumpster and it reminded me of my cat and the way the little thing had fought for its life the night I'd found her. I felt very much like the tiny kitten in that moment.

"You haven't begun to help," she said smoothly.

"But I did. I wanted to," I said again and reached behind me, feeling for the door. I wasn't sure why I was so scared, but I was.

"You visit the vampires. The vampires took her." The girl's voice deepened. A timbre of age crept in. "Therefore, you know where she is. And in the end, you will die to get her back."

All I could register was the word *die*. The rest of it, getting someone back, knowing where she was, trying to figure out who the 'she' even was? All just Scrabble tiles of words trying to be sorted into rational thought.

"That's how you'll help, you know," the girl said, as though I should have made that leap all on my own. "You're Ambrogio's flaw."

It was all I could do to wrest a question from my beleaguered mind.

"Who?" I said. "Who are you talking about? Who do the vampires have?"

"Morrigan," she said, looking annoyed.

She stretched her arms out to her sides. I fancied I saw broad wings stretch out beneath her arms, trails of black feathers hanging down and reaching for her fingers, and yet she remained the same 14-year-old teenager standing in front of me.

She met me, body for body as I pressed against the door. I rattled the knob behind my back, but it wouldn't budge.

She smelled of copper and wet dog. I could feel her heart beating against mine, but I knew my rhythm outpaced hers and the very fact that hers was beating so calmly taunted me. She was the aggressor. She was the one with all the cards. Her heartbeat proved it.

"Your death will set you free," she said.

And that was the thing that broke the protective glass of my fear. Without wanting to, I screamed. Loud. It hurt my ears and made my throat burn and I didn't stop to catch a breath even when she let go my arms and those hands of hers transformed right in front of me into birdlike talons.

She reached for my throat.

The shriek that erupted from her was a partner to my own, and I couldn't help throwing my hands over my ears.

A fold of feathers surrounded me, rigid but buckling as they enfolded my shoulders. I smelled the stink of old detritus and rotten meat.

The shriek of a crow overtook the girl's cries and even though I wanted to look at her, beneath the black darkness the enshrouded me I couldn't see anything, couldn't hear anything but that heartbeat.

I flat-out lost my shit.

I thrashed against the door.

I yelled. I screamed. I don't remember the feel of the door against my hands or my shoulders, only the way it finally flew open and the sense of vacant space felt like freefall.

I would have hit the floor of the bar with my cheek if someone hadn't caught me and pulled me inside. The door slammed shut behind us.

I couldn't catch my breath.

"What in the hell is going on?" Fayed growled.

I could barely focus through the dizziness. I struggled to master my breathing.

"I'm not sure," I murmured. I was intact, nothing broken, but I didn't feel okay. I lifted my gaze to his. "Didn't you see her?"

His brow crinkled in confusion. "See who?" without waiting for an answer he moved to pull open the door.

"No," I said, thinking that thing would be there, waiting. "Don't."

His hand paused on the knob.

"Don't go out there. She's mad."

I might have expected him to answer to that but a small sort of sigh from behind me caught my attention. I looked at Fayed as his eyes flicked beyond my shoulders. I knew by the expression on his face he didn't want me to turn around.

"Isabella," he murmured and this time he did look at me.

I felt something in my chest give way at the look on his face. Dread filled up the space it left, and I turned, slowly at first, giving him time to grapple me because I did not want to see what I knew I would see and yet I had to turn. Had to see what waited for me inside the bar.

Fayed and I were alone. Whoever his patrons had been, they were long gone. The girl who had delivered my water earlier, however, remained, if in body only. She lay outstretched on the surface of the bar, her feet, shod in sensible shoes, pointed toward the bathroom.

Her arms were flung to the sides and hanging off the sides of the bar. A long line of red fluid ran down the white skin of her bare arm. Her head strained so far backwards that I could see the deadpan look on her face, the last moment of living terror in her eyes.

Dead, my mind whispered. She was dead. I thought for a second it had been the girl from out front who had killed her. It would certainly explain the blood.

Then I remembered the thing outside was not human and not covered in blood at all, and I realized her killer was standing directly beside me.

CHAPTER 18

"I TOLD YOU TO never come back," he said as thought that was an apt explanation that made what I'd seen perfectly plausible and right as rain.

It was so much like Maddox's excuse that I spun on him with all the anger and fear I'd felt over the last hours.

Without thinking, I struck him against the collar bone with a tight fist and got nothing but a cracked and aching set of knuckles for my trouble.

"Fuck you," I said through tight lips trying to contain a sob. I felt betrayed. I'd trusted him. Trusted Maddox. Was there anyone in the world at all who hold up to a small standard of honesty anymore?

I was pissed and confused and terrified all at once and all I could think was my bug-out bag must still be there on the table and if it was, I wanted it.

I'd yank out the Ruger, the pepper spray, whatever the heck I had in there and I'd give him everything I had because this was not happening. Not today. Not when I'd already seen what I'd seen and lost faith in every other man.

And most definitely because that girl on the bar counter did not deserve to die that way, chewed on and drained of her life's blood.

Any other vampire, I might have just been disgusted or angry or afraid. But Fayed?

Words didn't describe how I felt.

"You fucker," I said because it was the only thing that seemed to convey it all.

I stumbled backwards to where I'd been sitting earlier, cradling my sore hand in the crook of my elbow. The pain was already subsiding, but I wasn't about to give in to the relief. Things felt too wrong to let myself feel okay. I couldn't feel better with that girl dead, with Fayed standing, looking at me like that.

I kicked around with my feet, trying to find the legs of the chair so I could collapse into it. I needed to sit before I fell.

It was in that search that I spied the bag beneath the table.

The legs were wobbly and spidered out from beneath the tabletop in five different directions. Even if I knocked my head on the edge and saw a dozen stars sear through the darkness as I dove for it, I knew exactly where the bag was. My fingers strained for the leather handle. I felt the belly of it brush against my fingertips.

I felt a sure, singular elation in that one moment of decision.

I'd get him first. Then I'd go for that creature outside whatever the heck she was and then I'd take out that damn fae, and then...

And then I just sobbed there underneath the table because if I'd learned anything in the last couple of weeks it was that I couldn't count on anything in the supernatural world. Guns, pepper spray, maces were about as useful as a whispered prayer.

Who knew? Maybe a whispered prayer was the best weapon.

Here I'd thought I had it all under control. Decision made. Easy.

Now I was lying on the floor of a vampire bar, throat deep in shit I didn't understand.

And I knew none of it could be fixed by a blast of pepper spray or a shot of lead.

I met up with Fayed's gaze beneath the table and he grabbed for my wrists, yanking hard enough that my chest collided with the legs and the wind hiccupped out of me. The bag skittered out of reach as he wormed his way beneath the table with me. The legs cut into my chest.

"It's not what you think," he said.

Damn if he didn't sound reasonable. I twisted away from him.

"Isabella," he said. "Look at me."

I squeezed my eyes shut so he couldn't compel me. "How can it be anything else?" I demanded.

He sighed and let go my wrists. "OK, maybe it's exactly what you think."

I peered out from half open eyes. He'd settled for hefting my bag over his shoulder out of my reach.

There was nothing left to argue with. No safety net. I was in freefall. What end could there be but the logical one?

"If you going to kill me," I said. "Do it now. I'm exhausted. I won't fight you. I can't."

It was true. I had nothing left in me.

I don't know how I expected him to actually do it. Maybe I imagined he would launch himself at me, teeth bared, his grip pinning me to the floor while he drained way the last bit of blood in my body.

What he did was pick up the table and throw it to the side. It crashed into the four piece setting nearby and the sound of it was almost too much. I cringed. I was exposed, lying supine on the floor where the table had been, chairs tumbled onto their sides around me.

My heart clogged up my throat, keeping the whimpers and sobs nicely stuck inside. No sound, my mind whispered. Don't make a sound. I peered sideways to catch sight of him, to brace myself for the inevitable.

I was going to die; that thing outside had said so. Because of a vampire.

Fayed was a roar housed in a trembling body. He was fearsome, terrifying. For a moment I thought he really was going to kill me. He looked down at me with an expression I rarely saw in a man's face unless he was about to do something violent.

I braced myself for impact, wrapping my arms over my head and tensing up.

Impact never came. Instead, I was lifted to my feet. The brush of soft hands whispered up my arms to my throat. He cupped the back of my neck, his thumbs cradling my earlobes.

"How could you think I'd do that, Isabella?" he murmured.

A chiding note under-painted the anguish in his voice. "If I wanted to kill you, you would have been dead the first time you stepped into my bar."

I felt a shuddering relief travel my core. I was alive.

It should have been enough to drain away the anger and the fear, but it wasn't. There was no good way to smooth over the girl lying on the bar with the last of her blood draining down her arms. How could he explain that to me? How could he make that right?

"You should leave," he said, letting his shoulders sag. He released me and turned his back on me.

Leave. The idea was laughable if I wasn't so terrified.

"I can't," I said and laughed out loud at the very thought. It was hopeless. All of it.

He looked over his shoulder at me. I noticed he aimed his body away from the bar, away from Ismé's accusing stare.

"You can," he said. "And you should."

"I'm serious," I said and crawled toward an upended chair.

He watched me pluck it from its side and put it to rights with a trembling hand. I scooted onto its seat and clutched the edges because I felt like even sitting down, I was too close to a razor sharp edge.

"What is going on, Isabella?" he said. "You were fine, things were fine not ten minutes ago."

His confusion was evident. I noticed he was making a point of keeping his movements as quiet and unassuming as his expression. No doubt he thought I'd lost my mind. Maybe I had.

I pointed to the door and noticed how much my hand shook. I eased out a long breath, purposefully trying to exhale the baddies.

"Out there," I said and hung over my knees, propping myself there on my elbows because sitting up just seemed like too much effort. "Then in here." I coughed into my hand because the words came out all scratchy. "Maddox." I waved my hand in front of my face. "All of it. Too much."

I eyed him. "Way too much."

I expected him to say something in response to the nonsensical statements, but what he did was go over to the bar and lift Ismé into his arms ever so carefully and carry her down the hall toward the bathrooms.

He had a back room, I knew. Maybe he took her there so her presence wouldn't bother him anymore. Maybe he felt guilty.

I let him go because I didn't have it in me to question it or to argue. Whoever she had been, whatever she'd wanted I had to either trust his truth or admit to myself that I was no safer inside than outside and I still didn't know exactly how much trouble I was in outside.

And that thought alone was enough to keep me pinned to the chair, staring at the door.

Inside seemed much better. Devil you know and all that.

I realized I was trembling and laid my palm on my stomach. Definitely in shock. I wondered how much more I could take before things shut down completely. I wondered how long it had been since I'd eaten.

I looked toward the bar, thinking maybe I could grab a couple of peanuts from a bowl and then remembered Ismé's body that had lain there.

I turned away, feeling as though I'd be sick. I hung over the table, tapping the surface with a fingernail until I heard Fayed pulling a bottle from the shelf behind me and pouring something into a glass.

When he approached me again, he slid a shot of amber liquid toward me. It wasn't food by any stretch, but I couldn't imagine a better sustenance right then. I bolted it back and set the glass back onto the table.

I ran my fingers through my hair. It was a tangled mess and it was sticking to my face from sweat.

He flipped a chair around and straddled it as he studied me.

"Start from the beginning," he said and watched as I waited out the burn of the whiskey.

And then I did. I recounted the creature outside and ended with asking for another bolt of whiskey.

He retrieved it and passed me a new shot glass.

"I've heard of the Morrigan," he said, putting an article in front the name. "I've never seen her, and I'm glad for that mercy."

He eyed me over the bottle of whiskey he held out to me.

I shook my head at the proffered bottle and he pursed his lips in thought. He was working something out, or at least trying to.

"Tell me," I prodded. "It can't be worse than me discovering my favorite vampire is a killer or that some of his buddies are going to kill me." I didn't mention how gut-wrenching it was to witness the things Maddox had done.

I kicked Fayed with my toe. We were far off from normal again, but the booze helped calm me, and that was something. I could even pretend there wasn't some strange creature outside waiting for me.

"No buddies of mine," he said. "I'm rogue." As though that would explain everything.

He sighed and stretched his legs out in front of him.

"What he knows about the Morrigan would fill a thimble," said a voice from the doorway. "What you need to know about her, you'd need to ask someone much older than Fayed."

I didn't need to turn around to know who spoke.

Maddox.

CHAPTER 19

I lifted my gaze to see him standing a few feet away. His hair was captured in its man-bun, wisps of russet clouding his earlobe where hair had escaped. His frame filled the doorway and I was reminded how big he was.

I hadn't heard him come in, and if Fayed had, he made no sign of it. His eyes were on me. Steady, insistent, just like Maddox's were. I had the feeling that both were waiting for my reaction.

Whatever Maddox had done to me had taken away the mental bruising and physical pain of my own beating, but the space left behind in my psyche left me uncomfortable. Like a critical part of character might have been dissected.

My belly quivered and something in my throat ached. I tried to tell myself it was fear, but my voice was surprisingly even when I spoke.

"You said we needed someone old," I said. "Someone like who?"

He shrugged. All these hours later, he still clung to that suit jacket he'd given me at the gala. It was slung over his shoulder and it slid backwards until he had to grab at it to keep it from falling off entirely.

I remembered the way it smelled of woodsmoke and whiskey and I looked down at my empty glass because for some reason looking at him just hurt too much.

"Someone as old as I am I suppose," he said. "Someone who knows the Morrigan when he sees her."

My head snapped up at that. He told me before that he was older than he looked.

"You're trying to tell us you're that old," Fayed said disbelief heavy in his voice.

Maddox ignored the question in favour of asking his own.

"Who is asking about the Morrigan, anyway?" he said, advancing into the room. "What do you need to know?"

"Isabella," Fayed said. "She just saw her outside. At least I think it was her."

"I didn't just see her outside," I protested at the way it sounded as though I'd just run into a long-lost friend at the grocery store. "I've seen her a couple of times. At the museum, on the way home from the Gala..."

"You saw her at the Museum Gala?" Maddox said. "Don't take this the wrong way, Kitten, but she was not at the gala."

"So says the ancient Morrigan expert," I spat out.

I waved my hand in his direction in a dismissive gesture that I hoped annoyed him. "You couldn't have been looking too hard or you don't actually know who she is after all. She was there I'm telling you. I saw her with my own eyes just like I saw her outside. In fact, I thought Scottie was using her at first to get to the curator, she was so 'there'."

"Trust me," he said. "I would know the Morrigan if I saw her."

I sucked the back of my teeth, indicating what I thought of that.

"Then why are you saying she wasn't? You had to have seen her. Pretty much the only teenager in the room, not counting the mummy."

I felt Fayed's hand on my arm. "Isabella," he said. "There's no point in arguing."

For some reason that was the last straw. I yanked my hand away.

I stood and faced Maddox. "I'm telling you I saw her. And if you knew her by sight the way you say you do, you would have seen her at the gala."

I was vaguely aware that my voice was raising in pitch and getting more shrill with each passing second, but I couldn't seem to jam the stopper back down on the opening.

I stabbed my finger in the direction of the door. "If you knew her, Maddox, really knew her or even had eyes to see, you would have seen her outside waiting for me because she is no more than three feet outside that exit."

Both men had the nerve to stand there looking for all the world like gentlemen awkwardly waiting for some manic woman to get over her hissy fit.

I wasn't done, though. I had one more bit of hiss left in me.

"So whatever connections you say you have with the supposed god, I highly doubt you're in the inner circle."

I wasn't sure why it felt so good to say that, but it did.

He took a deep breath and his gaze flicked toward Fayed and then back to me.

When he spoke his voice was soft and soothing.

"I do know her, Isabella," he said. "I know her well."

"Clotho, Lachesis, Atropos," he chanted, ticking the words off on his fingers. "Nona, Decuma, and Morta. The Celts are the ones who called her the Morrigan. She likes that one. At least, she used to."

I was nowhere near mollified by a diatribe of unpronounceable names.

"So which is she?"

He smiled. "All of them. None of them."

He ran his hand through his hair and I noted it shook a little. Maybe I'd struck a target he didn't expect, but that didn't sound likely. Something else was bothering him.

"She's far older than those incarnations, but they are all rooted in her somehow. The oldest of us know her when we see her. Humans, not so much. She's a shapeshifter. She can be whatever she likes."

I seized on that information as evidence of my senses and flung it back at him.

"She turned into a crow," I announced. "Right out there at Fayed's door. One great big crow with carrion stink on her breath and everything."

I shuddered as I recounted it. "If she changes shape, then maybe you just didn't recognize her at the gala, but she was there."

I crossed my arms over my chest.

He shook his head, stubborn. "There's one problem with that. She hasn't shown herself as the true Morrigan for centuries, let alone taken to a shapeshift."

I stabbed my finger in his chest. I felt like he was accusing me of lying, of all things. And tonight, I would not put up with it.

"That thing you say you would know on sight was right outside that door just minutes ago, washing my gala dress in a rain puddle. It was filled with blood. And then she accosted me. And then she told me I was going to die."

The last of the words broke on a shrill note and at the sound of it my fingers curled into a fist.

I felt Fayed's hand drop to my shoulder.

"I didn't see her, Isabella," he said.

His scent of patchouli and dish detergent wrapped around me. His hand where it lay wasn't warm the way a regular man's would be. It had heat, yes, but it was a sensation rather than radiant heat. It was another reminder that everything in this new world of mine was to be questioned.

Maddox took a step closer and I backed up into Fayed. If he noticed he didn't react to it.

"It wasn't her," he murmured. "It couldn't have been."

"But she was there," I said. I even stomped my feet. "She was."

Maddox shoved his hand into his pocket with a sigh and tapped his foot thoughtfully. After a few minutes, he moved toward the bar and reached over the counter. He hooked beneath it and came out with a tall bottle of absinthe.

With a lithe grace unusual in a man his size, he pulled his legs up and over the bar, and with the bottle of absinthe in one hand, he reached for the glasses with another.

Fayed did nothing to stop him when he slipped three fingers into three shot glasses and slid them one at a time along the counter at us.

"I'd say it sounds like the Morrigan," Maddox said.

"Thank you," I said and grabbed my shot glass. I felt very much like a celebratory shot was in order.

Maddox lifted his index finger along the bottle as he held it. "Except," he said. "There's two things wrong with it. One: she appears only to warriors about to die, and as difficult as you can be, Isabella, I wouldn't exactly call you a warrior."

We did agree on that, but I wasn't going to give him that satisfaction of saying it out loud.

"Two," he said, pouring a bolt of fluid into Fayed's glass but looking directly at me. "And this is the big one. It's not possible for you to have seen the Morrigan because she renounced those powers centuries ago. She's no longer the deity she once was."

"I did see her," I said. "Maybe I'm not a warrior, and maybe I'm not about to die, but I saw something. I saw her. She spoke to me. She warned me."

"Let's say you're right," he said. "For argument's sake. You saw the Morrigan herself, three times?"

He lifted an eyebrow for confirmation and when I nodded, he did too and went on.

"If it was her physical aspect, Fayed would have seen her. I would have seen her, and I know the form she takes." He gripped my wrist when he said that. "I do know her physical form," he said. "Trust me on that."

"Sure," I said sullenly.

He ran his thumb along my wrist, making me squirm enough to pull away and reach for the shot glass. I gave him a glare till he poured a shot into it.

I was aware of Fayed suddenly. Very aware. The way you feel when you've been caught groping someone when you thought you were alone.

I pushed the shot down to Fayed and he tipped it at me before downing it. I couldn't look him in the eye.

"So if we are to believe you know the Morrigan and that you don't think it's her showing herself to Isabella," Fayed said to Maddox. "How do you explain what's happening to her?"

He believed me. I could've reached out and hugged him.

Maddox didn't seem impressed at all. "I'd say that what she saw was the shade of the Morrigan, and not the true God herself."

"Rich," I said.

He rattled coins in his pocket. "The Morrigan is a three-part deity. Humans might call it a concert of body, spirit, and mind. When she renounced those powers those parts split. That cast of herself that she sends to warriors in warning has no real body anymore. No mind."

"That would explain why she seemed so insane," I muttered.

"Mad, more like," Maddox said. "It's a more sympathetic word. More sorrowful. And that fits far better for the circumstances."

He did indeed sound as though he felt every inch of that sympathy, and while I could applaud the sentiment in theory, I couldn't really feel the same way in practice.

"Right," I said in response, totally knowing how callous I sounded and not caring. "Because I should feel sympathy for a mad teenager who threatens to kill me."

He gave me a scolding look.

"If that's the case," I said, trying to backpedal without looking like an idiot. "Then where is the body? What shape does she take in human form?"

I said it as a dare, one I half expected him to take on, but I wasn't ready for the gauntlet to be picked up the way he did because I suppose I didn't really believe him until he jammed the right puzzle piece down into the picture.

"Haven't you figured it out already?" he said. "You know her."

He peered down into my eyes as though he was surprised I hadn't made the connection already.

"Kassie is the body."

CHAPTER 20

"That's not true," I said. "You're lying."

"Why would I lie?" he said. "Think about it Isabella."

Why indeed. None of any of this was making any sense, the least of it being a teenage girl I had been in contact with for three years being something other than human. It seems to me I would have picked up on it. Surely I'd have had some clue things weren't what they seemed.

Even as I considered it, I knew that I did have a few clues. No doubt I was just too stubborn or oblivious to pay attention to them. The strange demeanor that I explained away to myself as Asperger's or autism wouldn't alone have rung a bell, but when she had spelled me into the Shadow Bazaar to meet up with Maddox, that should have been a waving flag.

When she had pushed me out of the bazaar through that same awful portal and then disappeared when things had got heavy with the Fae assassin should have been a waving red flag.

Except I'd been ignorant about the otherworld and still flailing about for logical explanations for things that weren't normal.

I'd been too eager to assume she was like me. Regular. Normal. Human.

Just with very dangerous connections.

"Kassie," I said out loud. "It wasn't just because the portal was there waiting for someone to see it and use it," I said. "She opened it. She was the reason I was able to get through."

"The Blood Gate," Maddox said, his fingers halting mid air. "The most accessible for a mortal soul, if not one of the most uncomfortable."

I stared at him for a long moment, remembering my journey through that gate, the way I told myself I would never travel through it again.

"Blood gate because it requires blood," I said just making that connection too. "My blood."

He tapped his fingers against the bar. "And hers," he said. "The bond created between both, one vouching for the other, opens the portal."

"Why didn't you tell me before what she was?"

He shrugged diffidently but there was nothing casual about his gaze. It held onto secrets still. I was sure of it.

I remembered his reaction in his bazaar when Kelliope held her as captive collateral to flush me out and force me to give her the rune tile.

"When Kelliope found me there and used Kassie as a hostage and the entire bazaar was trying to free her, you told me she didn't need help."

I narrowed my eyes at him, as that whole scene loped through my memory. "You said she was fine."

"Not fine," he argued. "I said she didn't need you, and she didn't. Every single creature in the bazaar would have died for her if need be."

"But why?"

He traced a water ring on the bar, keeping his gaze carefully hooded. "Because they would hope she would be grateful."

I tracked his finger as it turned a water ring into a devil with horns. "Grateful?"

He nodded. "She has power over even the gods, Isabella. She might be broken, but she is the only one who can intervene with fate, change paths, she can even resurrect a soul if she wants to. If you could save the Morrigan when she's helpless or unwilling to save herself, you'd gain a powerful ally."

"And yet Kelly didn't care. She was willing to use Kassie as bait to get me to give up that tile."

He shrugged. "The Fae are not from this world. They're not bound by the same magics. Most of the creatures that move through the bazaar are of your world."

"And you?" I said. I watched him keenly for his reaction. I still hadn't figured out where he sat in all this.

"I care for Kassie. I have no need to curry her favor if that's what you're thinking."

It wasn't really what I wanted to know, or what I'd asked, but it answered a question that would have been raised anyway.

I watched him shove his hand in his jacket pocket, feeling around for something with a distracted look on his face as he waited for me to process it all. His cell phone, I supposed because he got a satisfied, relieved expression.

He scanned my face the way Scottie might, searching to plumb the depths of its expression. I knew what he'd see. Fear. Anger. Worry. All of them mixed together for a dozen reasons, not all of them based in concern for my own safety, but that was certainly there too.

"So what does she want with me?" I said. "Why do I keep seeing her?"

He shrugged. "She joined her blood with yours to get you through the blood gate," he said. "My guess is that left an imprint on you. Maybe her shade is drawn to that."

Something sparked in my mind like gears coming together with too much force and not enough grease. Something he was saying made those gears shift and change direction.

Far too many things had happened for me to just discount the evidence of my eyes and ears. Just in the last twenty-four hours, a sidhe warlord had broken into my house, taken the glamor off the building in a fit of vengeance. The museum had been targeted by something I knew was supernatural even if Maddox claimed it wasn't him. The young girl had been at that gala.

"You say Kassie is a god," I said carefully, and he flip-flopped his hand back and forth in answer.

"Sort of. She's a bit more than a god, but it's the easiest description for a mortal."

I was slowly piecing it together, letting the surprise lift away and leave in its place a wonderment that always came when solving a difficult problem. I let myself sort through the facts with mental fingers, sieving through the chaff that didn't fit the mesh.

Whatever was going on, it wasn't because I, a human mundane, was at the heart of it.

It was Kassie.

Whatever was going on, if this circumstance was a heavy weight, she was the fulcrum it all balanced on. The other weights, how heavy, how light, they needed to be put down in just the right order to keep it aloft.

I began methodically going over the talents. Kassie was a god. Kassie was missing. Kassie's shade had come to me in the only way it knew how.

"Could she have been the one that caused all the ruckus at the gala?"

His lips pressed together. "I doubt. She might have power over her shape at times, but not that kind of power...not being split from her triad nature."

"It wanted something," I murmured out loud. "She wanted something. She told me the vampires had her."

Fayed roused then and stretched his arms as though to encompass the room. "This vampire does not."

"Shh," I said, feeling for the invisible thread of fabric that would unravel the entire cloak. It was there. Right there. I just had to push my hand out into the darkness.

Strange that when I reached in, I felt the fur of my cat and the sound of glass breaking.

"He wanted me to find a god's bones for him," I muttered out loud.

"He, who?" Maddox asked, and I turned to him.

"What do you know about the sidhe?" I asked him. It was a new term and while I was getting more comfortable using it, I still didn't know what it meant. What they could do.

"They come from the ninth world, much like the fae do." Maddox waited for Fayed to toss a few peanuts into the air and catch them on his canines before he said more. "But they are not true fae. They are made fae. A hybrid of natural magic and human soul."

I eased my eyes closed to see the warlord again and heard him talking. "Colin, he called himself."

"You mean the fae who threatened to take the glamor off your apartment?" Fayed said.

"Didn't threaten," Maddox muttered. "He took it."

I could hear in his voice the reminder of finding me alone in my apartment, beaten to a pulp by a human man who shouldn't have been able to get in. As hard as the memory was, it overshadowed my fear of what he'd done to Alvin in return.

Seeing it all in perspective now, I wasn't afraid of Maddox anymore.

I felt as though someone had my back. And I needed that.

I inhaled deep, all the better to work through the threads. Sometimes things made more sense when all the other senses were shut out.

"It's connected," I said. "It has to be." I traced the pattern from the taste of blood in my mouth to the declaration that he needed me to find the stolen bones.

"Oh my God," I said. "It's her. The physical aspect of the Morrigan. The bones and body."

"What are you saying?" Fayed said.

I looked from one of them to the other, knowing for certain now what Colin was after.

"I'm saying the thing he's looking for, the thing he wants me to retrieve is Kassie."

CHAPTER 21

THE MORE I THOUGHT about it, the more certain I grew. If Kassie was some sort of god with her body, mind, and spirit separated, and if the sidhe warlord wanted me to find a god's bones, couldn't the two be the same thing?

"The real question is why does he want to help her?" I tapped my fingernail against my chin.

Maddox scowled at me. "If you're right, then you're saying vampires took her?" He leaned back on his stool, arms crossed. He wasn't buying it.

"I am." I couldn't look at Fayed because of what I was accusing his kith and kin of. It felt rude to look him in the eye.

"That shade out there was clear about it. She thought I was in league with the vampires. She even mentioned one by name. Ambrogio."

I laughed out loud then, because I finally made the connection. The satisfaction of piecing it all together made me thirsty.

"Pass me a shot," I said. "That was thirsty work."

Neither Fayed nor Maddox seemed the least bit pleased. One, russet-haired and man-bunned, looked like he'd eaten a rotten peach; the other looked like the last drop of blood he'd ingested had gone all clotted in his belly.

"What?" I said. "You act as though this isn't a momentous occasion. I can get my glamor back and help Kassie all with one act of kindness."

I lifted the bottle and poured the shot myself. I felt lighter than I had in days.

"*Slainte*," I said holding the glass up high before downing the contents with a smack of my lips.

I placed the empty neatly in front of me like a lady might.

"And how do you propose to do that?" Maddox said, leaning onto his arms across the bar and nudging the shot glass to the side with his finger.

I looked from him to Fayed, who for some reason wouldn't meet my eye.

I shrugged. "Surely one of you knows the name," I said. "You both being all supernaturally and all."

"You're drunk," Fayed said.

"Damn straight," I said with a grin. It felt good to feel so light. As though nothing was wrong at all in my little corner of the world.

Maddox sighed heavily. "The nine worlds are all big places, Kitten. No one knows everyone. Not even the supernaturally types."

I thought he was making fun of me.

"Minor problem," I said. "That's what intel is for." I scratched my head, excited now instead of nervous.

The sidhe had said he had intel. Now I wished I'd listened harder. I wondered if he would be inclined to give it now after I'd blown him off in favor of the gala job.

"How hard can it be to find a vampire?" I said and pointed at Fayed. "See? I wasn't even looking, and I found him."

Fayed laid his palm down in front of me and looked like he wanted to protest but Maddox shook his head at him, cutting him off.

"You plan to find a vampire," Maddox said. "One vampire out of all the possible vampires and do what exactly?"

"Well, not face him with a stake if that's what you're think-ing," I said.

"Oh, I wasn't thinking that exactly," Maddox said.

"I just need to find where he is, watch him for a while." I ran my finger along the lip of the shot glass. "A gal can't reveal all her secrets."

Maddox let out a short laugh. "Secrets?" he said. "You're about as lousy a thief as I've met."

It rankled. "You just haven't caught me on a good day yet," I said. "All this business with Scottie and sorcerers and shady bazaars with nasty things..." I sagged as I sat on my stool. "It's enough to throw the best of artists."

I thought he might take the time to argue, but instead he took the bottle from the counter and slipped it back under the bar. I caught him glancing toward Fayed and a secret look passed between the two of them.

"What?" I said. "I'm not so drunk that I didn't notice that."

"You've been far too sheltered," Maddox said and Fayed nodded in agreement. "You think because you come into this bar and leave again un-accosted that you have some sort of anti-vampire, anti-any-supernatural-creature aura?"

I squirmed on the stool. "No, but--"

Fayed gathered up the shot glasses. "Why do you think I told you not to come back?" he said. "This isn't a safe place. You're not safe here. Do you have any idea what it's taken me the last three years to make sure you leave here at night safely?"

"I hadn't thought about it."

"Right," he said. "Because you haven't needed to think about it. Because I kept you safely ignorant of the shade world. I let you in here, I fed you your favorite distraction laced with absinthe just in case you saw something out of the ordinary and needed a plausible excuse, and then I made sure every blood-sucking, flesh-eating, soul-drinking creature stayed away from you."

"Soul drinking," I said in a squeak. "Flesh eating?" I thought I felt dizzy.

He didn't answer but the look on his face told me everything I needed to know.

"Well I'm not safe from him now," I said. "I'm stuck right smack dab in the middle of it. So instead of telling me I'm not equipped to handle it, why not just help me?"

Maddox sighed. "All right, Isabella," he said. "Let's pretend you're right. Let's say you could find this vampire and steal into his lair and extract Kassie like some sort of military hostage. How would you find him in the first place?"

I shrugged. "Maybe I'll go outside and see if the Morrigan is still here. Maybe she'll point me in the right direction."

"Of course," Maddox said. "And then you'll run in to said place with a toy water gun primed with holy water and demand to see Kassie?"

I pressed my lips together. Most definitely making fun of me.

"Of course not," I said. "I'm going to steal her."

"Steal a living person."

"Yes."

"Alone?"

"Well yes, once I find out where this Ambrogio is. He must be in the city somewhere. You said vampires were human, from this world. He has Kassie. Kassie was here. It just makes sense to start looking here."

I hugged myself with the delight of not having to enter the Shadow Bazaar.

Maddox made a sound low in his throat that could have meant anything but that I took to mean I was being foolish.

I smacked Fayed's arm with the back of my hand.

"You must have contacts," I said. "Maybe you even know an Ambrogio."

Fayed got a strange look on his face. In fact, he'd looked remarkedly peaked since we'd turned the conversation in the direction of vampires at all.

"What?" I asked, understanding now why he looked so odd. "You do. You know who it is."

I jumped from the stool, not sure whether to be elated or angry. He'd been sitting there all this time with that information stuffed into his shirt.

"Tell me," I said.

"I don't know him," he said. "But I've heard the name."

His gaze darted toward the back room as he said that, and I remembered the girl on the bar, the one decaying out in the back room and I couldn't tear my eyes away from his. I felt, for one second, like he might lunge at me in self preservation. I reached for the bar to ground myself.

He must have seen my reaction because he laid his hand on mine.

"She asked for it, Isabella. She wanted to die."

This time when Maddox made a sound it was of disgust and if it was clear to me, it was to Fayed. I was gathering that he tolerated the vampire but no more. This coming from a man who let vampires roam his bazaar and buy children from witches.

I decided he didn't have a right to opine about them at all.

Fayed, however, seemed to think he did.

"I don't make a habit of drinking from an unwilling," he said to Maddox. "Although I do hear there is a robust trade in blood goods of all vintages."

This last was laced with an undercurrent of threat.

Maddox's hand curled into a fist on the counter. I knew he too was thinking about his bazaar and the barb had hit exactly where it had been aimed.

I cut through the air with a karate chop between them.

"So what's next? How do I get Kassie away from this vampire?"

Fayed sighed. "While it's not inconceivable that she's being held in a blood-letter's menagerie, I don't think that's the case. In fact, it might be worse."

My stomach knotted up at the term menagerie and flat-out squeezed at the thought there were worse things.

"What kind of worse?" I asked.

Fayed ran his tongue along his canines, obviously thinking.

"Wait here," he said and swung over the bar to head down the hall.

The tension in the air was palpable as Maddox and I waited for several long moments before Fayed appeared again. As he emerged from the shadows of the hallway, I caught sight of a familiar figure leaning against him.

They halted at the head of the bar and Fayed let her stand alone for one tension-filled second before she staggered. He was already catching Ismé before she fell.

I jumped to my feet, startled because I had expected her to be dead. A strange sort of joy welled its way up my throat. Not necessarily because I was happy she was alive but because Fayed hadn't killed her.

"You're not dead," I said and took a step toward her.

"I'm not dead *anymore*," she said and looked up at Fayed. Something swam across her expression that I couldn't quite explain as she looked at him, but I knew it didn't look like gratitude. Expectancy, maybe or entitlement.

I blinked stupidly for a moment, then realized exactly what had happened.

He had turned her.

Maddox must've assumed the same thing, but his reaction was much more decided. He muttered something unpleasant under his breath and I gave him a sharp look.

Fayed caught my eye and no doubt saw the communication, but decided it was inconsequential to the moment.

"Ismé was attacked by a vampire named Ambrogio," he said. "Repeatedly and viciously."

A look of anger crossed his face. "She'd be dead for real if I didn't do something to help her."

I eyed Ismé silently as Fayed fumed beside her. Something about the way she stood there, looking victorious instead of victimized, made me wonder what was going on behind that muddy gaze.

One thing was certain, she was strangely composed for a woman who had been attacked viciously before she'd had to turn to a vampire for help.

In fact, it was downright odd that she would have turned to a vampire for help at all.

"How do you know it was the same vampire?" I asked, although a name like Ambrogio was unique. I wanted to be sure.

"Tell them," he said to her.

CHAPTER 22

Sʜᴇ sǫᴜᴀʀᴇᴅ ʜᴇʀ sʜᴏᴜʟᴅᴇʀs in a way that was as deliberate as it was instinctive. It was a bracing breath, a final moment of decisiveness before plunging into ice cold water.

"No one calls him Ambrogio anymore," she said. " He doesn't like to be reminded of the man he once was and can't be anymore."

"Phantom soul," I murmured, catching Fayed's eye. He gave me a subtle nod of agreement.

She, however, canted her head at me, curious, as though she were studying me and trying to figure out what I could possibly know about such a thing.

"Like a phantom limb," I said to her. "Or so Fayed says."

She twirled a lock of brown hair around a delicate finger and pulled the ends into her view for inspection.

"Do you know what a phantom soul is?" Fayed asked her. "Many of us feel it."

He said it as though he was concerned she would stumble on it in the dark unexpectedly.

"If that means he still feels it, you're wrong," she said. "He feels nothing. He's focused on the same thing he has been since he was made by Artemis and Apollo."

She leaned against the bar in a weary way that had Fayed marshalling a stool closer for her. He seemed almost fatherly in his attentions and for a moment, I felt as though someone should divest him of the responsibility because she seemed to almost expect it and it angered me.

"You said he doesn't use that name anymore," I said, prodding her and forcing her to look at me instead of giving Fayed that entitled expression.

She swung her gaze to mine. "He calls himself Gio nowadays, the poor sap."

It was a strange way to refer to a vicious attacker, and even Maddox seemed to think so because he cleared his throat rather forcefully despite sitting there silently through the whole exchange. It made both Ismé and Fayed eye him.

"You say that as though you knew him before," Maddox said to her after running his gaze across her forehead like a neon sign might be there. "As though you've known him a long time." He gave her a narrow-eyed, suspicious look.

She ran her tongue along her teeth beneath her lips and gave him a direct stare. She didn't answer, but she didn't need to. She knew him. She had known him. Maybe longer than she wanted Fayed to know. It left me wondering if she'd been human when Fayed had turned her.

"Of course I know him," she said. "He's the one who's been chewing on me every night."

She thrust a now clear-skinned arm at him.

Maddox made a sound low in his throat. He didn't need to say he didn't believe her. Each of us could see that disbelief written across his face.

"Look," I said. "I don't care about your history with this Gio, or whether you knew him or know him and will know him. I just care about getting Kassie back, and you said you could help us."

"Kassie?" she said in a tone that implied she didn't care. "I didn't say I could help. I said my attacker was the same vampire."

Maddox was across the counter before either Fayed or I could react. I was left gaping at the blur of movement while Fayed lunged for him.

"What are you?" Maddox ground out.

He had Ismé by the throat and the woman didn't so much as flinch.

Fayed tried and failed to pull Maddox's hands clear. His canines extended out over his lips in threat and his eyes turned bloodshot and terrifying. Not exactly the kind of thing a gal wants to see when she's kissing distance from those teeth.

I couldn't get clear of my stool quick enough for my tastes.

The last thing I wanted was to get between a furious vampire and a complete unknown who had proven he could kill with a touch. And yet there I was, flapping my hands in the air at the both of them because I was too scared of getting too close and too afraid of what might happen if I didn't.

Fayed seemed the more rational. He backed up, but he was trembling. His hands were fists at his sides until he shoved them deep down into his pockets where they worked at his legs beneath, curling and uncurling.

"Stop it," I said, turning my attention to Maddox. "It doesn't matter, Maddox. Let her go."

"She's playing with us," he said, and the cords in his throat bulged. He was angry, all right. Mightily angry and yet a quick glance at Ismé showed a smirk lit her eyes.

She wasn't scared.

Unbelievably, she grinned beneath Maddox's hold.

"I'm a vampire now," she said. "I'm immortal." There was triumphant laughter in her voice. "Do what you will."

"Maddox," I murmured, tugging on his sleeve to get his attention. "Maddox, Fayed isn't doing so good."

It was true. The man I knew was gone and in his place was a feral creature who was obviously struggling not to attack. Some part of him inside was still the man beneath the creature, fighting for control.

Maddox seemed oblivious to the threat even when Fayed's lips curled back farther and I could see that what I originally thought were the kind of teeth of cheesy vampire movies made me expect were really a trio of canines on each side with a middle fang so sharp as to be the tip of a needle.

I shuddered and yanked a nearby stool in front of me as I backpedaled away from the bar.

Maddox gave him an almost lazy look and for a second, I thought Fayed was going to leap at him, fangs wet with saliva and deadly intent, but then Maddox held up his free hand, and uttered a word I didn't understand.

Fayed's chest heaved, his head swung back and forth. He snarled at Maddox.

But that was all.

Maddox swiveled his gaze back to Ismé who was still held in his grip.

Whatever the man was, I needed to keep in mind that he was strong. And able to control a vampire with one word.

Not someone I wanted to cross.

I gripped the back of the stool, not sure if any movement would change the dynamic. Then, Maddox let Ismé go and I watched as she ran her palm down the column of her throat, smoothing out the skin as though it were a silk collar.

Fayed wheezed out a breath and clutched at the bar.

I thought I saw his canines retract.

I eased out a slow, tentative breath.

"Tell us about Gio," Maddox demanded of her. "What is it he's after? Why would he have the Morrigan?"

That lit Ismé's face up with an almost perverse interest.

"The Morrigan?" she squealed. "Now that is a different sort of feast altogether." Her expression went dead for an instant as she contemplated the information. Just seeing the lack of life gave me the creeps, and when she swung that brown-eyed gaze to mine, I flat-out shivered.

"That bastard's crafty if not foolish," she said.

Fayed reached out for her shoulder with a trembling hand. Upon contact, he convulsed and gasped. I watched as the vampire shook himself back into the man as though he were a dog shaking off lake water from his coat.

"Sweet Jesus," I said because I knew I'd seen something few ever got to watch and still live.

"What do you know?" he asked her. "Tell us." The command was unmistakeable.

Ismé sighed irritably.

"You want to know what he's after?" she said. "His lover's soul, that's what."

She looped her arm around Fayed's back and I realized that it was that contact that was allowing Fayed to resume his composure. Maybe he needed to know she was okay.

Maddox still glared at her with a smoking gaze, but he kept his distance.

"And what does that have to do with the Morrigan?" he said.

She let go a nasty laugh. "You'll have to ask him," she said. "But be sure to wear asbestos underwear because you're going to have to go to hell to find him."

CHAPTER 23

IT TOOK ANOTHER SHOT of Rot Gut for my nerves to calm enough for me to settle back down at the bar while the creatures I was keeping company with circled each other metaphorically. I watched the showdown with trepidation, imagining that as Fayed exerted whatever influence he had over Ismé, she would eventually feed us the information we needed.

Maddox, on the other hand, did not make that transition easy or gentle. He glowered at them as Fayed cornered Ismé at the other end of the bar.

Whatever they were arguing over, it was making the hairs rise on my arms. I reached for the shot glass again, and was about to pour another drink when Maddox, whom I hadn't heard come near, laid his palm down over the back of my hand.

I gave him a sidelong look and he shook his head at me.

"She's thirsty," he said.

After the showdown between the three of them, with me, a vulnerable human in the wake, I was no longer feeling the least bit tipsy.

I wanted to remedy that right away. I pulled my hand out from beneath his.

"So?" I said. "Me too."

"Really thirsty," he said with a meaningful look.

I glanced at Ismé who was staring at me as she argued with Fayed. I noticed for the first time that the flat of his palm was square in the middle of her chest.

My stomach sunk as realization set in. "You mean?"

Maddox nodded. "He's telling her you're off limits."

"Oh my God."

"Has nothing to do with it, I'm afraid," he said. "She's bargaining with him. She'll tell us what we want to know in exchange for a sip."

I felt dizzy. "A sip."

He nodded and glanced at the door. "Sun will be up soon, so he better get her under control quick."

I noted he was scoping out the room with a scowl on his face. I took it to mean we wouldn't have another chance to get the information out of her.

In for a penny, in for a pound, I supposed. I wasn't all too keen on being Ismé's first blood hors d'oeuvres, but I didn't think I could live with being the kind of person who would leave a teenager, even a hobbled god, to the mercies of an unknown vampire.

Besides, I didn't even have my cat. She was lost to the fae warlord's realm, and who knew if he was feeding her or was just letting her roam my shadow apartment alone, aloof, and starving?

All of which told me I'd made the decision already. It was really all over except the doing.

And since the doing has never been the hard part for me, I took a deep breath and pushed back against the stool.

First step in a journey and all that.

I rolled up my sleeves and pushed off the stool. "Then let's get it done," I said.

He hooked my elbow from behind. "Are you sure?" he said.

I shrugged. I wasn't sure, no; but I knew there was no one else to do this thing. We needed Ismé's information, and I was the only human in the room.

"Could you live with leaving Kassie to the fates?" I asked.

His brow quirked comically. "Technically, she is the fates," he said. "And technically, I've lived through much worse. But that doesn't mean I'd want to live with myself if something happened to her."

"Me either," I said. I gave Ismé a lingering study, remembering Fayed's triple-fanged toothline. It wouldn't be pleasant, I knew, and I wondered exactly how much it would hurt.

I must have shivered because Maddox laid his arm over my shoulder protectively.

"I won't let her take too much," he whispered against my earlobe. "Just enough to get her through her first day of sleep."

I nodded mutely. I wished I could speak but for some reason, my throat felt all clogged up.

"Don't offer her your throat," he warned. "Just the arm."

"Okay." That came out alright, if a bit congested. I hoped I sounded brave.

I wasn't sure what the difference was except that one felt more intimate than the other. I imagined both would hurt and wasn't looking forward to either.

It didn't matter in the end. Fayed took the choice away from me when I told him what I planned to do.

"The arm," he said to Ismé, who nodded with an eager gleam in her eye.

Fayed glanced over his shoulder anxiously toward the back door.

"We don't have much time," he said, and I thought he meant I needed to hurry, so I thrust my arm beneath Ismé's nose because if a vampire says there's not much longer, I was willing to believe it.

"They're coming to roost," he said with a tinge of dread in his voice.

Even as Ismé's gaze tracked along my exposed forearm, a sound rattled the back-room door. Raucous noises like a crowd of teenagers coming home after a long night of illegal drinking pounded toward us. I shifted my gaze for one second, the same moment that Fayed and Maddox did.

And it was a second I knew I would regret.

Ismé grabbed me so suddenly I was yanked nearly off my feet and it was only when she buried her face in my neck that I realized Fayed was not worried about sunrise at all.

He was worried about the half dozen vampires who stormed the bar from the back door while we were still inside. He wasn't sure he could hold them back.

It didn't matter. It was too late for me to consider anything but the pain that streaked down my throat to my collarbone. I couldn't help crying out. I bowed over backwards under the force of her bite.

My entire body became a vacuum where all points of entry and exit were the same burning wounds in my neck. I felt her suction from the soles of my feet and I had the sensation that if I remained connected to her long enough that my skin would shrivel to fibrous husks and I'd be nothing but a shucked-out husk of flesh.

I heard nothing but the beating of my heart, doubled up with an echo of one other distant rhythm that grew in intensity for each pulse of the muscle.

Hers, I realized, climbing from a slow and frozen pulse to one that was hot with renewed force. I was filling her, I knew. Driving the beating of her heart with the electrical impulses of my own, the metallic element in my blood sparking it into movement.

The pain never ceased. Each pull was agony and I felt caught in a frozen scream that made no sound except in my own mind.

And then the screaming stopped.

There was a still, quiet space like the eye of a hurricane and I knew Ismé in ways I couldn't know without the blood bond.

I saw her with a lover, a mulatto woman of breathtaking beauty, who had called to her soul from the depths of some other world where she lay in wait.

She'd been dead already, at least three times, and in this one she shared the body she was in with another soul. Body thief, my mind whispered.

The spectre of my own psyche wound around hers and I could hear her laughter in the recesses of oblivion. Every time Ismé pulled in another draught of my blood, I saw more. I felt more. I knew her more.

She'd been a hell tracker, caught and kept by a seethe of vampires. She'd stolen for them, making their cult one of the most powerful. She tracked the most hideous and powerful of the supernaturals and caged them for her masters.

And who were those masters but the acolytes of Apollo.

Selene. A name pulsed with my heartbeat, echoing in my mind as though Ismé had spoken it directly into my mind. The original acolyte, the favorite of Apollo.

See her, Ismé whispered. Know her. She is the reason Gio is on your lips. She was his lover. The one who lost her soul because he stole her from Apollo and now every vampire is seeded in that bond that pits twin gods against one another.

I understood. Ismé was fulfilling her part of the bargain with each pull of my blood. But there was more. She hated the seethe.

She wanted her vengeance and her immortality. She was delivering the information she had in the best way she could, and I knew that the throat was so much closer to the mind and heart than the arm. The energy center, the chakra, just inches away.

Two souls lost to Hades. A curse that made of two lovers the first two vampires, taking their souls and gifting them to Lucifer.

Lost to a dark angel who loves his trophies as much as he loves himself.

And that was where Kassie was. Used by the male as a trophy to barter for the soul of the woman he loved still after all these eons.

I grasped it all in those seconds. How Ismé had found a way out of her own exile to Hades by offering a deal he couldn't refuse: the Morrigan.

She was the reason Kassie was in danger. She had baited Gio into abducting her and using her to barter Kassie for his lover's soul.

I groaned beneath the realization. Ismé had baited this Gio until he'd captured Kassie at the blood gate, using her bond to help me escape.

While she was vulnerable.

And now her spectre was trying to make it right, trying to reclaim the missing parts and was drawn to the only person on Earth that still shared a blood bond.

Me.

Then the pain of suction became nothing but the burning ache of a raw wound. Warm fluid ran a trackline down to my collarbone.

And the chaos around me swam into my consciousness like light flooding a dark room.

Maddox, my mind whispered. He had pulled me from the vampire's bite. The suction was gone, and he was gripping me by the waist and pushing me behind him. Yelling at me to wake up.

I blinked, trying to bring the room into focus. Nothing but a blur of russet hair met my gaze at first, then that full mouth of his came into view the way a magnifying glass makes things look crisp.

"Get out of here," he said.

Dumbfounded and stupid, I clung to him. I needed to tell him what I knew. I needed him to make Ismé pay for what she'd done. The suit jacket felt slick and wet in my grip. I swung my gaze to where my fingers still clutched the material. Blood. That's what was making the jacket wet.

My blood.

"Isabella," he said again, and I met his gaze. It was insistent.

"Go," he said.

And then I realized the chaos had erupted because Maddox was holding Ismé up in the air the way he'd done to Alvin. She dangled in his grip, limp but aware.

Next to him, Fayed was holding back the other vampires who had sensed their landlord wasn't quite himself and that there was a human in the room good for the taking. The stickiness of my blood made my throat tacky when I tried to wipe it clear.

One of the vampires lunged for me.

I stumbled backward, falling over a chair and spilling onto my hands and knees before I scrambled for the door.

"I'll meet you," Maddox shouted at me, and from above him Ismé laughed.

I ran for the door, with that laughter following me.

I ran for home. The cabbie didn't look twice at my bleeding neck, just took his cash and dropped me outside my brownstone. I paid him and ran up the steps.

Except in my haste, I'd forgotten why I'd left my house in the first place.

And I remembered it all with sudden clarity when Scottie, who was standing at my sink, swung on his heel to find me standing in the doorway.

"Sis," he said. "You're finally home."

CHAPTER 24

Scottie Lebans could freeze anyone in their tracks. He was heart-stoppingly handsome still, if a little chunky, the hard bands of unused muscle softening his torso. Women of all ages gawked at him, leaving their dates, their husbands, their kids in tow to pull at their sleeves to remind them of a sense of propriety.

Men might quake at his girth and muscled arms or knock knuckles in some macho ritual of acknowledgment.

But that wasn't all of Scottie. People genuinely liked him even if there was always a sense of threat emanating from him in waves. And for me, that was the worst of it; those who would lay down their bodies in service to a man they genuinely liked made the man himself all the more dangerous.

He'd paralyzed me with fear many times, and just as many sent me on a tear at full speed.

This time, he froze me at the door with his cozy sounding, I've-missed-you tone. Not one word about how he expected me to look beaten and bruised by his thug's hands. No apologies for sending the brute to my apartment in the first place.

I looked past him to my counter, half expecting the cat to be purring there but of course she wasn't. Only leftover plates I'd not dried and the stem of a broken glass left by Colin on the counter. Otherwise, my apartment looked much like it had when I'd fled. Socks still littered the floor. A jacket was slung over the back of a chair.

My hand on the knob spasmed as it tried to decide whether to yank the door open and send me running headlong down the steps again or find something to throw at him.

"Scottie," I said and was pleased to hear I'd somehow managed to match his cozy tone. Must have been all the other terrifying things I'd faced in the last twenty-four hours.

I swung the door closed with a finesse I was surprised to show.

"You're bleeding," he said and strolled across the tiled floor of the kitchen to meet me halfway.

He ran the back of his fingers along my throat, tilting my head to the side so he could inspect what he no doubt still thought of as his property.

Something bit you," he said. Study done, he gripped my chin between his fingers. His gaze tracked along the line of my forehead and to the other side of my neck.

"If that's all Alvin did to you, he wasn't worth his pay," he said.

He spit into his palm and rubbed at the blood. I winced at his touch.

"Bruised too," he said. "And yet that can't be enough to make you look so exhausted."

I nodded. I felt like a sack of dough that had risen and fallen too many times.

"It's been a rough night," I said.

He made a murmuring sound deep in his throat as he peered at me.

"Where have you been?" he said, as though the rough night was his to sanction.

I wrenched my chin from his grip and twisted out of his reach.

"None of your business," I said.

I aimed for the sofa because now that I thought about it, I did feel kind of weak. I didn't know how much blood Ismé had drained from me. Back in the bar it had felt like an eternity, but I know Maddox wouldn't have let it go on too long.

I guessed seconds, but even that seemed too long now.

Scottie followed me to the sofa and surprised me by lifting my feet up to rest along the length of it. He pulled a cushion from the chair and slipped it beneath my legs. He put his palm on my forehead.

"No fever," he said.

I eyed him from my reclined position, wary, wondering what he was up to.

"Rest," he said. "I won't be much longer."

"Much longer?" I said. I tried to see past him, but he filled up my vision as he leaned over me.

"I've packed the lingerie," he said. "At least the nicer stuff, but I'm leaving the ratty night shirt and jeans. The rubber soled shoes can come with us, of course, and the stealth outfits, but the rest we're leaving."

I sat bolt upright.

"You're packing me?"

"Packed," he said. "It's already gone. But that's not what we're waiting for."

The dizziness from the bloodletting aside, my stomach clenched into a dozen knots. I swallowed down hard, trying to decide whether or not I should ask.

"You have to be punished, Sis," he said softly, almost apologetically. "And not just for Alvin."

"Alvin is a brute," I said.

He nodded. "Alvin *was* a brute. It's what I paid him for. Of course, he won't be getting another paycheck, will he?"

I chewed my lip, waiting for the sweetness to abate because it always did.

"Where is your lover?" he said.

"My lover?"

"Yes," he said. "I know you didn't do that to Alvin. But somebody did. And you're going to tell me where he is."

With that, he extracted a switchblade from his pocket and flashed it within my eyesight.

My eye caught on the edge as the light caught it and it winked at me. I knew he wouldn't be showing me a blade unless he intended to use it. He didn't make casual threats.

Maybe I could talk my way out of it, but I still had to make it all the way across the living room to the front door without him getting hold of me.

That wasn't going to happen, but it didn't mean I couldn't try.

I tried to roll off the couch, but he laid a palm on my chest, pinning me flat.

"You are going to lie there until I decide you can get up. Do you hear me?"

I nodded and tried not to look too terrified. He would love that. But I wasn't foolish enough to think that my fear would mollify him.

He ran the knife up the hem of my shirt. The sizzling sound of it rending the material reminded me of the sound of my cat purring at the end of my bed and I wished suddenly that I had been more indulgent of her when Colin had been here.

I wondered how many other things I would be regretting in the next few minutes.

He spread the flaps of it wide, baring my bra and skin. He stared at my navel.

"You're trembling, Sis," he said.

He hovered his free hand a hair's breadth over my skin and I could feel the heat of his palm.

He caught my eye with his.

"I had a lot of time to think while I waited for the police to realize I didn't steal that coin. You had a ginger with you at the museum. Big guy."

He slipped the tip of the blade into my navel and the point of it skewered me deep within. One breath too deep, and it would pierce the skin.

"The ginger was tall," He went on. "But I doubt he could have done that to Alvin alone. Alvin was a big boy. A real warrior, but in the end, he was a mess. Three broken ribs, so my doctor said. Hemorrhaged out his left eye."

I swallowed down a rush of bile as I remembered it all. That had been me until Maddox had made his mojo on me. I still wasn't clear how he'd done it, but having the injuries listed out like that took away anyway residual distaste I felt for Maddox and left just a healthy respect.

And gratitude. Real, honest-to-goodness thankfulness. And for Scottie to list it all out as though the damage done to my body was nothing but an inventory for car parts made me hate him all the more. Of course, he wouldn't know that damage had been done to me.

I was whole and hale, and as far as he knew, guilty of inflicting horrific injuries on his employee.

"Alvin beat me senseless, just so you know," I said, catching his eye. "He beat me so bad I couldn't open my eyes."

Nothing but a lifted, and disbelieving eyebrow. Of course he wouldn't believe me. All that showed on me was the vampire bite that was bruised and ringed with dried blood.

"You sent him to hurt me."

"I sent him to teach you a lesson because I couldn't, being in jail and all."

"Some lesson," I said. "He nearly killed me. I should have let him so you'd see exactly how loyal he was to you."

Another quirked eyebrow, this time accompanied by a snort.

"Alvin wouldn't have beaten anyone that bad unless I asked him to."

"My point exactly." I glared at him, almost daring him to disagree.

"You need to understand," he said. "You are mine. Alvin knew that. Near dead I could take, but dead? He would know better. "

He sighed. "Your death would have to be by my hand, not his."

At that he leaned ever so gently toward my feet, holding onto the blade handle with the tips of steepled fingers. He reached for something from beneath the cushion and the movement made the knife tip bite into my navel.

I sucked back a breath through clenched teeth.

"Careful," he said. "That knife is sharp."

One jerking movement from him to the side and cold metal kissed the skin of my ankles, first the left and then the right. Cuffs, I thought. A long chain rattled between them with another set of bracelets, and it was snaking up my thigh as his hands moved upward.

"Give me your hands," he said.

He was going to hogtie me.

And then I would be at his mercy.

I couldn't let that happen.

"Wait," I said. The knife point was still in my navel and the sudden panic of tense muscles made it bite in, reminding me to lie so very still.

Scottie sighed.

"I gave you every chance, Sis," he said, shaking his head. "Every chance. No matter how many times Alvin told me you were no good for me I believed in you. I thought you would come back to me. To us.

"But he was right. You make me weak. I can't be weak."

"I'll come with you," I said, the panic rising. I would have promised anything at that point. The thought of being hogtied, unable to run or strike out was as terrifying as watching Alvin swinging from Maddox's grip.

"Just let me up and I'll come along. Just don't do this."

He shook his head. "Damn right you're coming with me," he said. "Just in chains this time. "

He heaved a belabored sigh. "I don't want to do it, Sis, but if I can't remind you why you are mine, why you belong with me, then everyone needs to see that at least I'm not weak. They need to see that what belongs to me always belongs to me. Never someone else."

Maddox again. Although Scottie didn't know the name of the man he thought of as his usurper, he was returning to the thing that bothered him the most. That someone else had taken his favorite toy.

"There's no one," I said, hoping I could appeal to his vanity. "No one since you."

"I wish I could believe that." He jangled the cuffs over my belly. "Now give me your hands."

CHAPTER 25

He rattled the chains, fully expecting me to obey. I had no intention of slipping my hands in between those cold cuffs. I needed to do something, anything to buy time.

"Please don't, Scottie," I said. "I'm sorry. I was wrong."

He canted his head to the side. He wasn't fooled, but he wanted to be. Deep down, he wanted to be so charismatic that he could persuade anyone of anything.

He laid the cuffs on my belly. They were frigid the way only hard steel can be. "Tell me who he is."

Giving him a name would serve only to infuriate him more and I knew that. It wouldn't be giving in to him, it would be admitting to him that someone else had tasted of his forbidden fruit.

"It wasn't a man," I said. "It was me. I had a weapon and I used it. Let me up and I'll show you where it is. I swear, Scottie. You know me. What kind of man would I expose myself, my truths to? You know I don't trust easily. You know me."

It was all the things he would want to hear: that he was the only man I'd ever trusted, that he was superior enough for me to be vulnerable with. Him. Only him. Always.

He appeared to be thinking about that. I could almost see him running through Alvin's injuries and trying to imagine what sort of weapon could do that to a man of his size.

"I was waiting for him," I said, hurrying along now with the story. "He thought he'd caught me by surprise, but I'd seen him following me. I waited for him inside over by the kitchen counter."

I jerked my chin toward the trashcan and the counter where there was an angle in the wall that could corner someone.

"I struck his ribs first," I said. "Knocked him flat onto his face. And then I swung over and over again before he could get up."

The thought of what I was describing made my stomach sick, but details were important. Especially to someone like Scottie. I tried to pull those details again to my memory, though each strike and blow was one I'd have died to protect from my cell memory.

"I kicked him in the stomach," I said, remembering how Alvin had driven his steel toed dress shoes into my belly. "And I was so terrified and so angry that I think I must have gone a little mad."

I let my eyelids shutter down at that. Shame and contrition. That's what he'd want to see, not the sense of vengeance that I knew gleamed in my eye.

"I'm sorry," I said. "But I couldn't let him hurt me. And then, when I knew you would come for me, I ran. I should have taken my lesson. I know that now."

He sat back on his heels. "But you came back here."

It wasn't exactly an accusation, but he needed to know why I'd return when he knew I expected him to find me. He was trying to add it all up in his favor and needed all the variables.

"Where else was I going to go?" I said. "You're going to find me no matter where I am."

"Damn straight," he said.

I had him. I just needed to press it all home.

"Plus, you were right about the museum," I said, hurrying to a sideline of apology that Scottie could understand well if he couldn't be swayed by the thought that I knew he'd find me.

If my terror of him wasn't enough, he'd understand two other things: money and greed.

"I found something there," I said. "Something that might mean an even bigger payoff. I just need your help to get it."

His face soured dangerously and for a moment I thought I'd miscalculated.

"So you came back because you want me to help you line your pockets."

I shrugged as best I could lying on the couch. Nice and casual. Truth looked casual, didn't it?

"It's as good a place to start as any, isn't it?"

A slow smile spread across his face. "It's the perfect place to start."

I could have wept for the relief.

"Then let me up," I urged.

He took his time retracting the knife from my belly button, but at least he lifted it out. I could breathe again. I sucked in air like I might never catch a breath again.

I waited for him to unlock my ankle cuffs, but he merely moved aside, Letting the chains dangle off the side of the sofa.

I tested the tightness of them by trying to flex my feet. Just enough give that I could walk, but it would be a shambling, awkward stride. Running would be out of the question.

"So?" he said. "Show me this weapon you had that could do that kind of damage to my best man."

"The cuffs?"

He shook his head. It was too much to hope for and I'd known it. With a sigh I swung my legs and feet to the floor. Sitting up sent a wash of black over my vision. Still dizzy. I had to wait a moment before my blood pressure equalized. I mentally cursed Ismé for the weakness.

"Waiting," he said from his spot on the floor.

I peered at him and nodded, and when he reached out to help me stand, I shook him off. I didn't want him to touch me. Not ever again. A trickle of blood ran from my navel to sop into the waistband of my jeans.

I knew there was no bat. No heavy piece of wood. It was just me in the apartment without my gun, my pepper spray. I couldn't run with shackles on. In moments he would know the difference and I'd be right back where I started.

I searched the apartment with a quick and surreptitious scan. There had to be something I could use. Something to gain me even ten seconds.

The glass winked at me from the countertop. Blue flashes like minute streaks of lightening pulsed in ways that reminded me of the sidhe's eyes.

"Hold on," I said. "It's in the broom closet."

I shuffled as best I could toward the kitchenette. Scottie followed along behind me, close enough that I could smell his cologne. Good. Let him get good and close.

There were two rather large shards pointing up from the glass bottom, right about eye width, that had his name on it.

My stomach ached from the knots it had tied itself up into. The tiles felt cold on my feet. He'd pulled off my shoes and socks so I couldn't run even if I got free. But he'd forgotten I'd run in my bare feet before. I could steel myself to pain if I knew it was a vehicle to my freedom.

"One question, Sis," he said from behind me before I got more than five paces away from him.

I was almost there. I tried to measure from his voice how close he was. Maybe I could reach out for the glass, spin around and stab him with it. That might buy me enough time to get out of the apartment, but run too far with the shackles? Not going to happen.

I needed the key to the cuffs. I needed about three minutes from the time I stabbed him to the time I jammed a key in the lock.

It wasn't possible. I looked over my shoulder at him, afraid that he would have his switchblade pointed at me, ready to lunge and hold the point of it at my throat. For a big man, he was incredibly athletic. He'd managed before to backhand me across the face and still catch me before I fell.

"Yes?" I said, making sure to infuse the word with all the meekness I could muster.

"You explained how you killed him," he said. "But I still have one question."

The glass was just a hair away from my right hand; I could see it in my peripheral vision. The broom closet knob at least a foot. Would he suspect anything if I moved too suddenly?

"I didn't mean to kill him," I said, thinking he believed the desire to take something away from him was the problem, and trying to explain the accidental nature of it. "I just wanted to stop him from hurting me."

He clutched the material of my flapping shirt, holding me fast. His expression spoke volumes in what he believed and what he didn't, and it was filled with distrust.

"Yes, you said that. But how did you drag him all the way to my hotel room and dump him at the door?"

He scanned me from head to heel. "You're not strong enough, not big enough for that."

The material of my shirt tore loudly as he yanked me hard back toward him. Whatever I had hoped for in terms of time, my moment was on me. There was no thinking. No rationalization. I just twisted at the same moment, reaching for the glass with straining fingers.

There was no time to consider where I stabbed, I just stabbed.

I expected him to scream or strike out in pain.

But he disintegrated in front of me, turning to ash in the air.

The glass melted to nothing.

An illusion, I thought at first, but only because the shock made me stupid. I knew it couldn't be true. My shirt, the blood on my stomach, the shackles cutting into my ankles all told me it had all been real.

I didn't dare move. Everything was the same, right down to the way the faucet dripped at regular intervals into the sink. The socks on the floor were the same. The blood spots on the floor, leading a trail to where I stood were the same.

All except the way my cat was coiling about my legs as though she hadn't seen me in weeks. The sound of her purring throttled through the air.

That was how I knew I wasn't alone, and I was not in Kansas anymore.

"The glass," I said, making a guess and aiming the words to the room. He would hear it of course, the sidhe warlord, because the smell of toffee wafted around me.

"You made it into a portal."

I was speaking to empty air, but I knew he heard. The cat's constant purring was evidence he was near. I knelt to scoop the cat from around my leg and held her in front of my face, watching where she looked. Her gaze flicked to my shoulder and I dropped her to the floor and spun, awkwardly, with the sound of chains rattling, toward the counter.

He sat on it, swinging his legs. Boyish.

"I'm right, aren't I?" I said, trying not to act as though I was surprised even though I didn't expect him to be right there, so close to me. "It was the glass."

"Smart human," he said. "But it's not a portal. More like a key."

There were a dozen things I wanted to say to him. A dozen things to accuse him of and rail at him over: the Morrigan, the loss of my glamor. Scottie breaking in. Alvin torturing me.

All because of him.

"You lied to me," I said. "You told me a seethe of vampires stole the bones of a god and you needed me to steal them back."

He shrugged. "Body and bones is what I believe I said. That was no lie."

"Well, vampires didn't take her. Just one did."

He lifted his eyebrow. "Indeed."

"You said it wasn't a goose chase at all. You said it was my life or death."

"Another truth," he said.

"It's an impossible task," I said. "I call that a goose chase, one I can't win. I could never get the glamor back and you knew it."

"It wasn't glamor," he said. "I was clear about that. If it was glamor you'd still be fighting off your lover."

He'd watched us, I realized, and past the fury that he still called Scottie my lover, I was incensed that he'd let it all happen without a single intervention. He'd seen every torturous second of Scottie staking his claim. I swallowed down the frustration in favor of getting to the bottom of the issue.

"So I'm here in the fourth world with you? And Scottie is in the ninth world, and your relic, your goddess of bone and body is in Hell."

I threw the last at him spitefully. He couldn't retrieve her. No one could. I nearly sobbed on the knowledge that it was Kassie, poor thing, who was stuck in that world and she couldn't be reached.

"Yes," he said. "I do know that. You'd have known too if you weren't so myopic."

"Well I can't very well lift her out of the pits of Hades," I said. "So it wouldn't have mattered."

"And why is that?" he said with an almost comical slant of his head.

"Because I'd need to be dead, is why," I said.

He grinned, showing me those crystalline teeth again.

He pulled a velveteen pouch from his pocket. Elegant fingers that held the hint of a callous or two ferreted their way within to extract a piece of jewelry with a very large setting.

He tossed it at me.

I caught it without thinking and peeked at it as it sat in my palm. An amulet of some sort, sans the chain. An ivory snake swallowed its own tail as it curled around a teardrop made of burgundy amber.

It would have been a magnificent enough artifact alone, but what made it even more intriguing was the symbol trapped inside that looked itself to be traced out in blood.

"It's gorgeous," I said, and I had time to look back up at him before I felt my chest squeeze tight.

My lungs felt like they were on fire. My eyes stung like someone had dropped acid in them.

"You said you needed to go to Hell," he said amicably as I gaped at him through a wash of tears. "No problem."

And then the squeezing in my chest turned to pain, and I couldn't breathe.

I fell to my knees, the shackles around my ankles striking into my calves and then twisting my ankle as I fell to my side.

I might have felt relief that the shackles broke free of my legs and fell to the floor with a noisy clatter, except everything started to tunnel down to one small prick of light that made me realize he hadn't been kidding at all.

I was dying.

CHAPTER 26

Death was wet and warm. Very much like what I imagined a womb might feel like.

I floated in death, liquid heat ebbing about me and lifting my limbs. I'd gone to the Mediterranean once with Scottie and tried to submerge myself in the salty water but instead bobbed in it like a cork.

This was a lot like that. I could remember the way I'd tried to open my eyes under water and the sting of salt that bit into my tear ducts until I'd had to squeeze them closed.

The thought of being submerged, of opening my eyes, made me realize my eyes were closed. I gained some sense of proximity of my limbs right then.

I understood that a crushing sense of pressure had gathered in my lungs.

And that was the moment when the serenity of death ended.

I was not breathing.

And I needed to breathe.

My lungs burned with it. I'd gone too long without sucking in oxygen and every tissue in my body demanded it.

Surely my lungs would constrict at any moment. Surely my chest muscles would expand, my mouth would open, and I'd suck in deliriously brilliant air.

And when they finally did, I fought the inhalation because some baser instinct past my befuddled brain and aching lungs told me breathing was the absolute wrong thing to do even though it was the thing my body most craved.

Not that it mattered.

My lungs contracted on their own as though to spite me. They sent a pulsing tremor through my tissues that forced my mouth open, the thirst for air so great, I gasped.

Of course I pulled in water. Hot, lung-drowning water that tasted of soap.

I struggled against the sudden onslaught of liquid. In the blink of a synapse I remembered that death should not be hot and soapy like old dishwater.

Death should be dark, aching even. Not wet.

That could mean only one thing.

I was alive.

Wherever the damn sidhe had sent me, it wasn't to hell.

And I would be dead in seconds if I didn't find my way to the surface.

I fought whatever it was that had me tight in its grip. I thrashed about, trying to find the surface. I coughed, spluttered, tried to expel what I could even as I twisted and reached with straining fingers above me.

Something tangled in my hair and yanked. Real, tangible fingers knotted the locks and used them as a handle as it pulled.

My scalp burned with pain.

Whatever had me by the hair was dragging me along the water. I struggled against its grip and thrust, scratching out, biting down. Kicking wherever I could. More water invaded my mouth as I tried to protest.

I could hear another heartbeat in the water, drumming along with my own.

I struck out with feet and hands. I thought my toes touched bottom for one second, that my fingers found air. Thank god and the angels, I thought I found purchase. I was ascending.

In the next heartbeat, I was coughing up hot water and soap was running out my nostrils like a lava flow. Everything from my lungs to my sinuses were on fire. I blinked, trying to squeeze the water out of my eyes enough to see.

My hair hung wet over my eyes and bled water down to my mouth. I coughed again, drooling up the last of the soapy water onto my chest. I struggled to find the edges of whatever I'd felt that I had fetched up against and when I did, I wrapped my arms over the lip, hanging on and trying to see where I was.

"How did you get in my bath?" said a masculine voice. It sounded deep and throaty and masculine.

Something hiccupped in my chest. The dread and ridiculous hope that the voice was Maddox's died as quickly as it surfaced. I didn't recognize the voice at all.

Bath he'd said. I reached out on both sides and my fingers fingertips touched metal on the left and right. A bathtub, yes. A deep bath. Like a swimming pool. I reached my toes down toward the bottom and found that I could just barely scrape the bottom.

"I said how did you get in here?" he said.

I clawed my fingers across my eyelids and brushed the hair out of my face. I peeled my eyelids open despite the soapy burn that made them water all over again. I blinked too fast and too hard to get a good look. The blindness disoriented me.

"Where am I?" I said in a shrill voice. "Who are you?"

I heeled my palms into my eyelids, frantic to be able to see.

Whoever was in the tub with me, had an iridescent sort of glow to his skin, and an aura that traced his body like those old-fashioned medieval paintings. I thought I could make out silvery white hair. Two of the blackest eyes I'd ever seen were inches from my face.

I started, not expecting them so close and sent a ripple of waves to splash against the sides. I bobbed against the rim.

I tried to propel myself over the side, but I couldn't get enough purchase with my toes. I could feel the water moving again, larger waves lifting me higher as he swam toward me.

I thought I could make out the faint throbbing sound of a heartbeat all around me. I knew the sound of ragged breathing could not be mine because I had the feeling I was still holding my breath.

"Am I dead?" I said.

"Not dead, apparently," he said.

I clung to the side with both arms flung over the edge. I hung there as the water buoyed me back and forth until it went still enough that I could look sideways at the person who was with me in this oversized tub of hot soapy water.

What sat on the other side of the tub like a gargoyle hunkered down in a steaming Roman bath was a man at least triple my size. His chiseled pecs rose above water level and flexed and twitched under my scan.

If I looked just the right way at him, the glow around his edges was reminiscent of the illuminated text in books scribed about the medieval saints.

But I knew this was no saint, and I knew it as soon as my feeble brain slipped all the puzzle pieces into place.

"You're the devil," I said.

An arrogant smile formed on his mouth. A beautiful mouth. One that was thick and pensive.

"I prefer Lucifer," he said.

Angel of the morning. Of course. He looked very bright indeed. His beauty was heart stopping.

"And who are you?" he said as he leaned toward me, laying the tip of his nose against the skin of my cheek.

I froze as he inhaled and dragged the tip of his nose down along the column of my throat and beneath the water toward my chest.

At least I was still dressed, if clothed in tatters of a shirt from my visit with Scottie. The flaps of my shirt were still hanging from my sides and I felt Lucifer's nose fetch up against the cup of my bra beneath the water.

I had the feeling he might try to bury his nose beneath it much like a dog might. But he didn't. Instead his head broke the surface of the water again. He regarded me with suspicion and something that looked like unexpected delight.

"You're not ethereal," he said with a note of wonder. "I think you might even be human."

He said that last with a tentative gasp that made me shiver. It pleased him, this information.

"Mortal," he said in a whisper.

And then as though he surprised himself with this news, he laid his hands over both of my breasts atop my bra. One palm covered half of my chest. He squeezed ever so gently, testing.

"Mortal, alright," he said. And his tongue ran along the bottom of his fleshy lip.

I knew the sound of lust in his voice. The sound of possession. I'd run from it, made a life for myself with the note of it haunting my nightmares.

I'd come all the way to hell just to hear it again.

No way. No fucking way. I wasn't going to be someone's possession again. Not even Lucifer himself. I didn't care if I'd come here willingly to try to help a god escape hell.

I didn't care if I had to promise the devil my first-born child to get back home. I didn't care if I had to kill Scottie to keep him from me forever.

I. Was. Not. Doing. This.

I moved to crawl out of the tub. He caught me and wrapped both arms around my waist. They were pythons of muscle, broad and undulating as he pulled me against him. Water sloshed up my throat and went up my nose.

My legs swung free between his as he stood to his full height. I was molded to his chiseled frame. Water sluiced down my back.

As massive as he was, I was no more than a child's toy against a full-grown man.

With a deft movement, he scooped my knees from beneath me and wrapped my legs around his torso. He buried his face into my neck as I felt him step up and over the edge of the tub.

Busy hands began trying to peel the clothes from my body as he strode across the floor, but they must have proven too small for his huge hands and fingers. He had to tear the shirt from my body. It fell backwards off my shoulders.

The air in the room dried my skin immediately.

I was stunned. Terrified. My brain incapable of forming any other realization except that evidently, Lucifer was a horny little devil.

I knew one other thing, and it streaked across my mind with crystal clarity.

I had to get free.

CHAPTER 27

I BEAT AGAINST HIM and he chuckled darkly. Obviously, he knew I couldn't best him that way. He was too strong, too big. Instead, I thrust myself backward, arching as far as I could and as suddenly as I could.

That, he wasn't expecting. My feet swung free of his waist, since my legs weren't long enough to hook behind him and I fell onto the hard floor.

I lay on my back with the wind knocked out of me for too long. He was already advancing toward me, his naked body glistening from the bath.

He was magnificent, yes, but his size was terrifying. I tried to roll onto my side and push myself to my feet but couldn't move. I was left trying to gasp in a gulp of oxygen as my eyes tracked his progress toward me.

Behind him squatted that swimming pool he called a tub. It was half buried into the floor the way a hot tub might be. A magnificent copper thing with ornate decorations along the side. Close inspection might prove them to be demons cavorting with angels, but I wasn't about to get any closer to it than I was already.

Even with me a few paces away from it, and with it sunk into the black and glassy tiles, he was able to close the distance in one tread.

I was riveted with horrific fascination by the sight of his member, engorged and standing.

Panic bit into my throat. I held my hand up in surrender.

"Wait," I said. It had worked before hadn't it? With Scottie?

"Wait, I need to catch my breath."

He stood over me, the water sluicing from his skin and dripping onto my face. I blinked, as one of the waterdrops landed in my eye.

"You're not ready for me?" he said, confused and agitated. "Why else would you come to me here if not to please me?"

He sounded ridiculously entitled, but I stuttered out an explanation, something about not knowing I was even on a journey let alone to please him. I apologized. Three times.

He reached for a plush swath of material that appeared just within his reach, hanging in the air as if from an invisible peg. It was big and broad enough to cover my recliner chair, but in his hand, it looked like a regular sized towel. I was beyond relieved when he lay it over his hips, covering his massive erection and freeing my gaze finally.

I thought I could breathe again.

"You didn't want to come here?" he said. "How odd."

His gaze tracked over what was left of my sopping clothes and dripping hair.

"And how disappointing."

I let go a breath of relief at the statement. I didn't know what he expected of me and my visit, but I was sure I wasn't ready for any of it.

He crossed his arms over his chest. The monumental pecs flexed and let go.

"So," he said. "You want me to wait; I will wait. It's not every day a living mortal descends into my paradise. Take a few moments to recover yourself."

It was as good as I was going to get, I supposed, and it was enough for now. Enough that I could take in my surroundings and search for an exit or an escape route if I needed. I had a reprieve, even of a few moments, and I wasn't about to waste it.

Without my shirt, and my jeans yanked half off my hips, I could feel a pulse in the floor beneath me. It wasn't just heat, but a warm heartbeat that thrummed deep within its core and coursed hot blood through large and small veins every direction.

My palm ran along the surface and found it smooth like glass. Black in spots so deep there was no reflection. In some spots rough as though hewn from hardened lava. But all over it was warm. I felt my skin drying even as it heated the air around me to an almost uncomfortable temperature.

The walls were covered in paintings of apples in various states. Some were large, some small. Every colour and shape of apple was depicted, some of them bitten into and some of them whole. It seemed to be a theme. One that he revisited over and over.

I tried to hitch up my pants over my hips and felt better when they covered my backside.

"You are recovered?" he said as he noted my scrutiny. "You're ready to tell me why you're here if not to service me?"

I tried to get up and failed. The shock and after effects of Ismé's bite, I supposed, coupled by seeing Scottie, then being throttled through what I imagined was a portal threshold much worse than the Blood Gate at the Shadow Bazaar.

I tried not to think about how I was going to get back out again even if did manage the sidhe's mission. Because surely that's why he'd sent me here. The knowledge of it burned in my throat. I was never likely to accomplish let alone survive. And he knew it.

"I was sent here," I said. "Against my will."

He made a thoughtful sound deep in his throat.

"I shouldn't be here," I went on. "I need you to let me go."

"Let you go?" he said.

"Yes." I started to add that someone else was here as well, someone who no doubt had found herself trapped here who didn't ask to come, but he crouched down next to me and propped his elbows on his knees as he regarded me.

He laid his thick index finger against my lips. It took up three quarters of the width of my mouth.

"No one asks to come here," he said matter-of-factly.

He scooped me to my feet so that I stood in front of him, looking up and feeling terribly small. I crossed my arms over my chest to cover the barest parts of my breasts not covered by the demi-cups of my bra.

His eyes dipped to my navel then back again to my face. I had an image of him running a long, slug-like tongue along his bottom lip and yet, his expression remained carefully placid. I shivered involuntarily despite the heat.

"Let me show you my Paradise," he said, and the undercurrent of his tone reminded me of slick and dark places where moss grew, covered in cobwebs and murk.

I followed his gaze with mine to track along the room. The lighting seemed to come from everywhere and it washed everything in red. Whether or not it was from lights or its natural hue, it made the walls look drenched in blood.

"I have a labyrinth," he said proudly. "One that doesn't get appreciated nearly as often as it should."

He looked down at me with the boyish pride. "I'd like to show it to you."

"But my reason for being here," I started to say but he cut me off with a sharp look.

"Many people think hell is nothing but a burning, agonizing plane made up of fire and brimstone," he said as though I hadn't interrupted him. "But it becomes what you expect of it. I can make it whatever you want. I can make it whatever I want."

He slipped his hand over the small of my back and at his touch I felt a tremor move through my entire frame.

A thousand images kaleidoscoped through my mind's eye. I felt grief and pain all at once and then it was gone, and I was just padding along next to him, helplessly led toward a shadowed area that the blood-red light didn't touch.

As we moved across the glassy floor, shadows lifted one by one as though some master lighting expert was illuminating tableaus in a theatre.

"First," he said, aiming me toward a wall that seemed to go along toward a far-off horizon. "You need to see my collection."

We drew near a wall lined in artifacts large and small, weapons interspersed with arcane objects like chalices and goblets. They seemed arranged aesthetically rather than by purpose.

While a human collector might have shelves filled with curios, pottery, even wineglasses supported on wooden shelves or hung with decorative hooks, his were desiccated hands and feral creatures' jaws, and they clutched weaponry of all sorts or balanced trinkets on pointed teeth.

"Aradia's grimoire," he said, pointing to a vellum-bound book before moving on to point to other objects in turn. "The helm of terror, Merlin's staff, the Ripper's blade." He sighed with longing. "I haven't touched that in decades."

"They're mine," he said in a tone that would have caressed each piece if it was a touch. "Acquired over millennia."

He reached out as though he wanted to touch the knife but held off just a hair's breadth away. He moved his hand to the left and lingered over a spear large enough to fit his hand perfectly. Whatever it was, it had to be owned by a giant.

"The spear of mortal pain and death," he murmured. "Hewn from the bones of the greatest sea monster of your history. In your ninth world, the spear would need to be stored in a vat of water; its heat is so great it would spark fire in stone. Here, however, it rests as though it has always craved the quenching my heat can bring it."

He let his hand fall to his side and turned to face me. I knew he was looking directly at me, expecting me to be impressed, maybe even expecting me to show him with round eyes of awe exactly what I thought of it all.

I couldn't meet his gaze. Instead, my eye rested on that hideous spear. I couldn't imagine something like that coming from my own world or imagine the man who might have wielded it.

"You've collected all of these?" I said. "And all from my world."

"I collect things that interest me," he said. "This spear is especially relevant to your plea of escape."

He touched my cheek, forcing me to look at him. This time, that slug-like tongue did run along his bottom lip and he didn't try to hide it. I thought I might faint.

"I don't usually get living mortals here," he said in a lowered voice. "In truth, I get ethereals. Well," he shrugged diffidently. "I always get ethereals. They are better suited to service me because they don't get broken."

The way his eyes ran over my skin made it crawl in response. Every hair lay down flat against my skin, as afraid, it seemed, as I was beneath that gaze.

He swallowed slowly, convulsively and when he spoke again, it was with a husky, throaty timbre.

"Without the risk, where is the excitement?" he said and let his head fall back and closed his eyes.

I took a single step backward, not sure where I would go but instinctively wanting to be as far away from as I could be. His hand snaked out and gripped me by the wrist, holding me steady.

"It was a man last," he went on inhaling as though the air was the memory of it and he couldn't get enough. "A Welsh warrior whose mastery over that spear was legendary. Oh how he fought me. He was strong and very bright. Beautiful to behold."

He crushed my hand in his massive one.

He looked me over and despite the heat I went cold.

"Surely you see that I'm not in the business of letting things go," he said.

Now I understood exactly why Colin hadn't come himself. He knew what I hadn't and what I was only just beginning to understand.

There was no way out of hell.

He clasped me by the hand and pulled me more than led me toward one of the more shadowed areas. We passed the tub and I bent to scoop my shirt from the floor as we passed by. I pulled it over myself as best I could and clutched the tatters together over my chest.

"Come," he said. "You must see my menagerie. I've set it all out like a safari. You'll enjoy it."

"The labyrinth," I guessed, and he laid a finger against my temple, tapped it twice.

"Smart," he said. "Even if you are quite small," he said, inspecting me. "I could carry you in my pocket."

He seemed to show some delight at that and although it was a strange sentiment, especially in light of the fact that he was still naked, I pretended to be impressed.

"Do you have any vampires?" I asked coyly.

He sucked the back of his teeth. "Vampires don't exist down here. Their human souls are mine, given up in their death. The body stays on earth. But the ethereals that they are here belong to me. I can do with them what I want. Even barter and trade them if I can find a buyer who has something worth the eons of pleasure I can get from them."

"I'm guessing that doesn't happen often."

He murmured his excitement that I was a smart little human soul. "It has happened less than a dozen times in my whole existence." His chest puffed out. "But I recently bartered three of those souls for something far greater."

I couldn't hide my excitement. Gio and his lover. Ismé as well. And that had to mean a connection to Kassie.

"Can I see this thing?"

He looked so pleased with himself that I might have pitied him had he been human.

"In time," he said. "But first you must see the menagerie."

The way to the labyrinth took us deeper into his boudoir. I never got the sense of movement or distance, only the feeling that things were changing. They altered subtly at times and at times one pace seemed a hundred.

Statues rose up out of the shadows to meet my gaze. Struck in every sort of action, frozen in different positions, some of them obvious states of sin, nude and life-sized. And surrounding them, as though to reflect a desire to recreate their tableaus were recliners, lounges, beds, and swings.

The array and variety boggled my mind. Flickers of movement caught the periphery of my vision. They were moving, the statues, but each time I gazed straight at them, they froze again, and it was disconcerting to always feel as though the world around you moved while you remained still.

"How do you like the mirrors," he asked at one point, and I'd not realized he'd placed full length mirrors in strategic places.

I peered into one to see he and I naked and entwined together on a bed of coals. I sucked in a breath, sudden dizziness making me sway on my feet.

He looked down at me and tugged me toward him. I butted up against his waist and felt the heat of his skin. He thought my gasp was of pleasure, the egomaniac.

My heart hammered against my ribs and the sound abandoned my ears as I swung my gaze from mirror to mirror.

In them all, we were engaging in sex. And most of them looked absolutely terrifying. Some of them looked flat-out dangerous. In three of them, I was obviously dead.

He wasn't just a horny bastard, he was a psychopathic one.

My knees turned to wet sponges and I stumbled, catching myself from falling only because his hand was still wrapped over mine and he tugged on me like a yoyo to keep me upright.

I hung limp in his grip, a bobbing bit of wood on a slack string. I sagged against him because for the life of me, I couldn't put any steel in my thighs.

I wanted out. My core began to tremble enough that it shook my shoulders. My teeth clattered together.

"I'm not supposed to be here," I stuttered out around the clacking of my teeth. "This was a mistake."

I pulled in hitching breaths, aware that I was hyperventilating. My whole body should have shut down by now. I prayed for it.

"The best is yet to come," he said. He sent me an indulgent look. "And the most interesting. Come. It's what I really want to show you."

He tugged on my hand and we continued. I took in the way the shadows retreated from his step to reveal the door to what he called his labyrinth. It was gnarled and twisted with a material that faintly resembled paper mache vellum. There were streaks here and there branching off into small, cobweb-like tributaries. Much like veins.

"Is that--" I started to say, and he nodded as he put his finger across my lips.

"Flesh?" he said. "Oh, yes." He looked delighted that I recognized it. "But the real treats lie beyond the door."

With a bracing breath, I stepped inside and as I did, the door disappeared behind me and all that was left were dozens of thresholds ahead of me and Lucifer standing beside me with an anticipation so palpable it goose pimpled his skin.

"I've been down these hallways hundreds of times," he said. "But since you're my guest, I'll let you plot our path."

So he wanted me to choose.

I remembered somewhere reading that right-handed people usually turned toward the right, and I imagined he knew that as well. Best to keep him off guard. Besides, if I kept always going forward, then I would stay in the middle-of-the-road. Metaphorically speaking.

"There," I said, pointing to the middle.

The same fabric that made up the door made up the walls as they stretched up past me and out of sight into the shadows.

I had the almost irresistible urge to run my fingers along the surface and reached out for it.

He grabbed my hand and held it back.

"Not yet," he said. "You're not ready."

He squatted down next to me so he could be level with my gaze. With his black eyes pinned to mine, he lifted my hand to his mouth and ran that tongue along my palm. Every muscle in my stomach clenched. My knees buckled, and I tried to yank my hand away.

He held it fast, stared into my eyes.

And then he bit down on it.

CHAPTER 28

I SHRIEKED IN PAIN, but no sound came out. I panted, my chest heaving.

"Now you're ready," he said with a flick of his silver hair.

He spun me around like a kid playing pin the tail on the donkey and ended with me facing the wall of flesh. Close up, I could make out pools of prismatic light beneath the tissue. He let go my hand and I cradled it against my chest.

"Look," he said and waved his arm across the wall. Those pools of light peppered the surface. They went up and on past my line of sight.

"Those are ethereals," he explained. "I have millions of them." There was a sigh in his voice.

He looked down at me with pride in his expression.

"Sometimes I take them out," he said and pulled my hand to the wall, where he planted my palm on one of those pools.

"Blood is how you choose," he said.

At that, something shuddered beneath my palm, seeming to press against the skin. I yanked my hand away, but too late, whatever had brushed against the wound had begun to take shape in the wall. The prism bulged out from the tissue that held it and it grew arms and legs, a torso, a head.

A man erupted from the wall's skin and the grotto where we stood turned into a forest filled with black earth and spruce trees with broken branches.

The man blinked at us as though we were smoke. He rubbed his eyes.

The stink of scorched foliage and sulfur filled the air. Shells exploded overhead, light assaulted the air.

The man my blood gave birth to ran toward one of the trenches. Clothes wrapped around his naked form as he ran, streaking for a pile of dirt. He jumped in.

"Watch," Lucifer said.

He snapped his fingers and the rather small onslaught of sound and light became chaos. Screaming and yelling rent the air and I watched as the man from the wall tried to climb out of his trench and escape the clutches of a man with a bayonet who'd stabbed down into his back repeatedly.

I doubled over in response, unable to keep my stomach from hurling up its disgust and fear. Everywhere I looked that same man was dying a thousand different deaths by thousand different hands. Each one of them more grisly than the last.

Instinct made me cringe closer to Lucifer and the heat of his body wrapped around me. He pulled me close, enjoying my fear.

"Oh how I would love to put you in my pocket right now," he murmured. "But there's more I want you to see."

He laid his palm on another pool of prismatic light and this time the grotto shifted like a haze across hot asphalt and transformed into a vacant lot with cement bedding. Unlike the man who had birthed himself whole from the living tissue of the wall, this one streamed from it like lightning toward the centre of the grotto.

I noticed he held something orange in his hand. A large can, I thought, reminiscent of gasoline cans.

The man sat cross-legged in the middle of the cement and upended the can over his head, letting clear liquid stream down over his body. Too late, I realized what was about to happen. I didn't turn my head away fast enough before the man lit a match and was engulfed, screaming, in flames.

Lucifer's shoulders moved in what I presumed was a disappointed sigh, but I couldn't hear it over the shrieking as the man was consumed by the fire.

"He is my least favourite," Lucifer said over the. "Because even though he can make his torment what he wants, this is what he always chooses. It's too fast. Almost as soon as it begins."

He held me close, the palm of his hand running down my back to cup my buttocks.

"You're trembling," he said. "Does it excite you too?"

"Why are you showing me all this?" I asked.

"You want out of my domain, do you not?" he said.

He'd already said he didn't let things go. And it was obvious that whatever else Satan was, he was also a lecherous hoarder, feeding his paradise with people's torture and torment. Relishing every bit of pain and anguish.

No wonder Gio wanted to save his lover from this place. No wonder he wanted his soul back so badly. I thought of Fayed and how he'd said vampires had phantom souls like phantom limbs and I wondered if this was what they felt. This torture happening to their souls over and over for all eternity.

And Kassie. If Ismé had been truthful, Kassie was here somewhere suffering too. I wanted to think I was the kind of person who could push cowardice and self-interest aside, but I was a thief. I didn't care about anyone else but myself.

It was a humbling thing to realize, but all I could think of was that one of these was going to be me and it terrified me. Whatever pity I felt for the poor girl, my own sense of self-preservation was paramount. I hated myself for it, but I nodded at him with hope clawing into my chest.

"I do," I said. "I want to go home."

He smiled. "Don't worry," he said. "My domain is one of death. It's a matter of time before you return. A foregone conclusion, if you will. Just like my Welsh warrior, living mortals have no place here."

That was a relief to know. I wasn't stuck here forever. I was a mortal body being lent a bit of time here in Hell by some magics I didn't understand. No doubt the sidhe warlord had bought me that time with the talisman I'd caught as he'd tossed it to me. I didn't have it now. For all I knew, it was at the bottom of Lucifer's tub.

"What happened to the Welsh warrior?" I asked, because it had to mean something that another living soul had descended to this realm.

"He broke," he said with a shrug. "He was only mortal after all. Still living and breathing when he came to me. One of my hell hounds was attracted to him; the warrior had this natural affinity for dogs and beasts of all sorts. The hellhound thought I might enjoy him and collected his body for me before he expired and released his soul."

He spread his hands behind his head as he arched his back. He looked like he was flexing for a sparring match.

"You saw his weapon in my collection. The spear. A magnificent thing, unique in all the nine worlds. I had to have it. When he came to me, it was with the weapon clutched in his hand and when I saw it, I wanted it. I ordered him to give it to me. He refused to relinquish it."

"So you fought him for it?"

"Oh no, I made him fight because it pleased me and his body was mine to do with as I wanted while he was here."

He glowered down at me as much to say I was his possession as well. I tried not to hug myself like a coward.

"But you have the spear," I said, imagining the kind of man who would refuse Lucifer. He would have had to be massive. Brutal. Primal and strong.

"Yes," he said. "I broke his body, alright, but he stabbed me. It's really a horrific weapon that must be cut free of its host. Mortals can't survive it."

He ran his hand absently along his belly as though reliving it, and I noted seven wide scars criss-crossing the flesh that I hadn't noticed before.

He sighed. "I broke his body for his insolence, but his soul was not mine to play with. He wasn't quite all the way dead. Just...broken. Of course I couldn't return him to your ninth world. He would never again be the same."

I felt uneasy. The pieces of the puzzle started coming together as though magnetized. So I could return, but after Lucifer was done with me, I likely wouldn't be the same. But where would I go? How would I be different. I needed to know.

The sheer thought of it, made the space between my ears swim. I had to hold my arms out sideways as I momentarily lost my balance. His gaze slipped over me, assessing me in one quick second before his expression went carefully placid again.

"And which world did you send him to?" I said. I had this odd sensation of detachment, like nothing mattered even though I knew I wanted the answer.

That speculative look again. One split second of interest and then nothing.

"The fourth world, where he could be made whole again. With magics to fill in the places that would never be the same."

The fourth world. The world of the Fae and magic. A warrior who wouldn't give in. There was something there, but it danced just out of reach.

"I had to send him back, but the spear was my trophy in lieu of the soul. And he agreed to leave it on pain of forfeiting his ethereal self to me should he enter again to retrieve it. And I hoped he would. I so hoped. For centuries, I've been waiting for him to use my talisman to return for it."

My heart stopped at his mention of a talisman. Again, that dancing of puzzle pieces trying to fit together.

He peered down at me again with that look of keen interest. It felt like he was looking through me, somehow digging into my past and seeing everything that was there. I fancied he could pick up the moment I clutched the broken glass to stab Scottie and was transported to the fourth world.

Instead he sighed longingly.

"I'd broken him, you see. And as I said, few gods have the magic to regenerate."

His expression lightened suddenly. "I have one of them here, you know," his eyes gleamed like mica stones. "She was a steal of a deal, actually."

I stared at him for a long moment, thinking I should feel something about that information but I was still struggling to find the picture in the puzzle. I knew he meant Kassie. He had to. And yet I had to struggle to bring to mind the appropriate question.

"Can I see her?" I asked.

His lips thinned out for a long moment as he considered it, then he shook his head.

"Time is growing short for you," he said as he sent his gaze up and down my frame. "I dare not wait any longer to put you to service. I've already wasted too much time."

"Service?" I said.

"You are mine, remember?" he said. "For the time you are allotted here, you belong to me and I can do whatever I want with your body and bones."

He waved his hand over the air and it wavered again, shifting the grotto into something of his own making.

I was mortal. I was his possession now. But I, like the warrior, would also break. Far too soon for his liking. I tried not to think about the war scenes, the battle he'd had with the Welsh warrior, because if I did, I was sure the grotto would shift into something horrific.

"Am I going to have to fight?" I squeaked out.

"Oh you're not built for fighting," he said.

I swallowed down hard, knowing whatever he said next was not going to make me feel better.

He snapped his fingers and the grotto became a deviant den of carnal pleasures, decorated with S&M accoutrement and equipment of every imagining.

"You, my living soul, are built for something else entirely."

CHAPTER 29

I BALKED AND STUMBLED and if he noticed it, his dark chuckle seemed to indicate he enjoyed my discomfort and anxiety.

He was a collector. Collectors liked to talk about their collections. He'd already wasted much of my time already doing that. Surely if I showed enough interest, he wouldn't be able to help himself. I had no idea how much time I had. As far as I knew his idea of it being short might mean a century.

"But how could you have got this god in the first place?" I said, stalling. "A god wouldn't let herself be bartered, and surely not for a couple of vampire souls."

"Human souls," he corrected. "Vampires are bodies without souls. Those souls are mine."

I put my hand on my hip, indicating I didn't believe him. "You want me to believe a god was fooled by a vampire into becoming part of your collection."

He scowled. "I have no need to lie."

I pursed my lips. "In my world, you are called the god of liars."

"I'm misunderstood in the ninth world," he said. "I don't have to prove myself to you. Remember, you are mine, not the other way around."

"So I'm guessing that means you don't have one," I said. "A god, I mean."

His face darkened. He bristled and with a swipe of the wall, without touching down on the liquid pools, he shifted the entire landscape so that all that was in front of us was a panel made of tissue.

Behind, I knew was his wall of collectibles, his armoury, as he'd called it. To the left was his gargantuan tub. The right corner lay shrouded in shadows. My feet felt stuck to the glassy tiles. I did not want to know what lurked in those shadows.

"Behold my god," he said with a flourish in his voice. "I traded for her. A vampire came here with her and all he wanted was two measly souls. Old ones at that. He has no idea what a bargain I struck."

Kassie, I realized. No longer body and bone but something different, something that lent a pale blue light to the room. She certainly looked like herself, just more of a shell. As though someone had stretched plastic down over her body and molded it to her even as her essence evaporated.

Without animation, or real veins and flushed skin, she looked more like an empty husk than a teenager in stasis.

Quicksilver ran out from her husk in every direction. I ran my gaze along one of those veins, and realized they branched off into different places, stretching all the way around the living tissue in the wall.

He sucked the back of his teeth as he studied her. "She's only a shell. The other parts are detached and in your ninth world."

Detached and in my world. I thought of the Morrigan and her haunting sort of madness. Had it been exacerbated by a phantom soul being tormented here?

"Have you used her?" I said, although I was terrified of the answer.

"Absolutely not," he said. " She is very much like your world's Star Trek merchandise."

He laughed at his own joke.

I ran my hand a hair's breadth away from the surface of the wall, not wanting to touch it because I didn't know what would happen to her if I did. I didn't want to risk whatever was here would stream out into the space and end up enduring some horrific tortures.

Instead, I traced the veins of mercury along to the outskirts where they turned from arteries into veins and then into smaller branches that looked like cobwebs throughout the wall.

I guessed that whatever essence was in her body was here. I could see the bones that made up her skeleton and they were graceful and delicate.

"She's quite something," Lucifer said from behind me. "Although I still don't know how she would let herself be led here by a vampire. The lowliest of breeds," he said with a curled lip.

He looked at me for a long time. "She should have known better."

"Because she's a fate?" I said.

A slow smile spread across his face. "The fate," he corrected, and his pride was evident in his voice. Like any collector he was eager to talk about his acquisitions.

"You said you traded her for two vampire souls," I said. "How is that even possible?"

He jerked his chin in her direction. "Like the vampires, something is missing from her. The vampires' bodies are in the ninth world while their souls are here. Her body is here but..."

"Her spirit is elsewhere," I said. I knew it was true. But he didn't know I knew.

He nodded hurriedly. "You understand," he said.

"But how do I know she's real and not just someone like me? A human body you encased in some sort of magic husk to fool your guests."

"As if I had to fool anyone. A true collector doesn't fake trophies," he said with a growl.

I shrugged. "Aren't you afraid I'll touch her like the others and release her?"

He laughed. "She's not some ethereal to be commanded by human blood at whim," he said. "The only thing besides my touch that can release her is a strong connection. Any of her other triad selves, for example." He looked over his shoulder as though checking for them. "And they aren't here, now, are they?" he asked me.

"No," I murmured. They were not. Just me.

I peered at her. She almost looked as though she could see what was happening. Despite the shell and the lack of blood and bone, she seemed aware and sentient and my throat ached to see her like that. I'd found her alright, but I was powerless to help her.

Even if my time did finally run down and I returned somehow to my apartment, Colin would never return my glamor.

It was all for nothing, and now I had to worry about returning to that realm whole and unbroken, a feat that even the Celtic warrior hadn't managed.

As far as pickles went, this was wasn't just sour, it was rotten.

Even if I somehow managed to get home healthy and hale, I'd no doubt have the Morrigan's hounding me till I died because of those damn few moments Kassie had taken my blood to spell me through the Blood gate.

Hopeless.

Or was it? I stepped closer to the wall, tracing her face with my eye. She was the Morrigan's body, after all, not powerful, but the aspect of the god that connected with me strongly enough to get me through the Blood Gate, to have her shade chasing me through the city.

"What about a blood connection," I said. "Would that be enough?"

He scoffed. "What blood bond would there be after all these centuries. She renounced her powers, hid from the world and from humanity. That isn't even her true form."

He said that like he felt disdain for her and it made me angry.

"No," he said with a slightly inflated chest. "I'm the only one who can release her. But I'm not going to do that."

"Because you don't want to take her out of the package," I said, unable to keep the sarcasm from my tone.

"Exactly." He looked at me with a smug expression.

"Why, though?" I said. "Why give up all that to be alone for centuries and end up here?"

He shrugged. "Mortals," he said. "Why else?"

He heaved a sigh as he looked me up and down. His black-eyed gaze lingered on the gap between my shirt where I had the feeling my demi cup had slipped.

I tugged the shirt tails together over my chest.

"They're a weakness," he said. "Common as rats but so uniquely made. Fragile, but strong-willed. Stubborn. Passionate. Entitled."

I shifted uncomfortably beneath his gaze as he trembled visibly.

"She fell in love with a human warrior," he said. "But he rejected her. Such a pitiful story. She tried three times to make him fall in love with her. The history of your ninth world records the flavor of the story if not the true tale."

He jerked his chin toward his armoury shelf.

"The spear of mortal death and pain was his to wield, which makes having her all the more special."

Now I understood why he displayed them together. The only thing that seemed to be missing was the warrior himself.

And that's when it hit me. What he was trying to tell me.

I peered up at him to see that smug look had changed to one of excited pride. The collector had impressed me, and he knew it.

Except what he thought had impressed me was that he had two of the three items in one spot, and I was remembering that he lost one.

And I knew exactly where that third piece was.

My sidhe warlord Colin was the selfsame Celtic warrior Chu Chulain.

"Now," he said abruptly. "We've wasted just enough time."

He peered down at me in a way that made me swallow convulsively.

"Time to put you in my pocket," he said with a languid smile.

"You'll feel some pain, I admit," he went on. "Actually, quite a lot judging by your size, but I can make it so you enjoy the pain if you please me."

I was horrified to see that in the moments I'd been studying Kassie and putting the puzzle pieces together, he had lifted the shadows of the corner to the right.

Like a magician whose lighting engineer specialized in sleight of light instead of sleight of hand, the corner revealed aspects that were as viscerally terrifying as they were disturbing.

Costumes of leather hung from pegs and each of them looked meant to restrain its wearer. Complete vinyl suits designed to encase a person from foot to ear hung next to ropes and leashes. Various equipment, swings, and tables squatted in nooks and crannies like toads. A shelf of whips and cuffs and masks.

I broke him, he'd said of Chu Chulain.

Chu Chulain. Colin. The sidhe warlord who announced his arrival with the taste of blood. A god bound to me by blood.

My stomach knotted and my legs went weak.

I had one chance and I couldn't waste it.

I bit down into the palm he'd broken earlier, and the taste of blood filled my mouth. Copper and zinc and salt puckered my cheeks as I drew hard on the skin, pulling out whatever I could, wincing beneath the pain.

"You enjoy pain?" he said with a tinge of wonder in his voice. He sounded as though he'd hit the jackpot.

"Hell no," I said.

I pressed my palm down over the tissue of the wall, stretching my fingers to meet Kassie's as it lay on the other side.

For one long agonizing moment nothing happened. I'd been wrong. I'd failed, and now I was stuck here until the talisman ran out its time and sent me home.

I prepared myself to swing around and face Lucifer. But then just when he reached out for me to pull me away from the wall, a jolt of energy went through me, throwing him backwards. The tingling against my palm buzzed.

Then it burned.

And then the tissue of the wall contracted and with a horrific sound, wrapped around the empty and transparent shell of bones on her side of the wall.

CHAPTER 30

Lucifer let out a tremendous howl from behind me as he crashed into his collector's shelf and dozens of artifacts crashed down onto the floor. His was a howl of fury and despair and I imagined he grieved all the hours he'd spent arranging those awful relics of humanity.

And then Kassie stood in front of me.

"The talisman," she said. "Where is it?"

The sounds of wailing reverberated around us.

"I don't know," I said. "The tub maybe,"

"You have to think," she said. "Time is running out."

"I know," I said. "I've been doing my best to stall him."

"He's lying," Kassie said. "You think you're running down the clock, stalling him until you can be brought home again," she said reaching for and clutching my hand. "But it's him who stalling. He's running down your clock until the talisman runs out of the power to send you home."

I should have seen it before. He'd already told me that he'd given Colin the talisman. Why would it benefit anyone other than Lucifer? I'd been foolish and stupid to not see through the ruse.

"It's in the tub," I said. "It has to be."

"Take us there," she said.

I didn't understand what she meant. The tub was right there, just a hundred yards away. Surely she saw it.

Howling reverberated around the room. I could hear Lucifer climbing to his feet amid the clutter.

I could hear his breathing, a heavy, chugging, locomotive kind of sound coming from behind me.

"Hurry, Isabella," Kassie said. "If you can't take us there, bring it here."

Bring it here. Lucifer had said earlier that his fire suicide kept performing the same act over and over even though he could do what he wanted with this torment. He'd said hell was the torments people made.

I imagined the tub, what it felt like to be drowning in that hot soapy water, feeling Lucifer's thighs around me.

Seconds passed. A single heartbeat pumped within my chest and then suspended there, as though it couldn't finish its movement. I couldn't catch my breath. Kassie's hand clenched in mine, squeezing the fingers together.

"There," she said. "There it is."

And there it was. For a second, I felt the joy of victory.

It was short-lived as I felt Lucifer's hands tangle in my hair. He tugged me backwards and I stumbled, letting go Kassie's hand.

"I've got you," he said.

She looked terrified, small and waiflike. The tub was right there. I didn't have to see it to know that the talisman sat at the bottom of its copper base.

"Go," I said. "Just go."

She gave me one long look, sad and resigned at the same time, and then she spun on her heel and leapt for the tub. She climbed over the copper side and dropped into the water with barely a splash.

All sound was gone into a vacuum for several long moments as Lucifer tightened his grip in my hair and let loose an awful howl. He shook me in his fury.

"Now you've done it," he said. "You lost my treasure."

He hoisted me by the hair to dangle in front of his face. My scalp screamed with pain and I felt several clumps of it come free. Before I dropped from his grip, he wrapped his fingers of his other hand around my throat and held me there.

The face that had been handsome turned to something feral.

"She left you here," he said, and a smile twisted his mouth. "Selfish bitch if you ask me," he said. "But at least it means you're mine now. Really mine. For all eternity I will make you suffer for it."

He pinned me with a hateful gaze. "You gave your timepiece away." He laughed, and the sound was nothing like it had been before. Cinders and ash must have clogged up his throat because his laughter was black and ugly.

"You relieved me of that infuriating need to drag out your time. Now I don't need to suffer those niceties to keep you talk talk talking and yap yap yapping insufferable things and questions that mean nothing."

He threw me to the floor and loomed over me. "Just pain," he said. "Lots and lots of pain."

The shadows were fully lifted now. The room was washed in painful light, almost gleeful in its clarity. The relics and artifacts were still strewn about the chamber but beyond were things past the human imagining.

If it had ended with bondage equipment, I might have understood what was about to happen, but when I caught sight of an archaic looking rack, I realized this was going to go so far past violent assault and move into the realm of torture that I knew sanity wasn't going to be an option.

"Mine," he said again. "For all eternity." He eyed me greedily. "No talisman to take you home. No need to worry about breaking you."

He giggled. Actually giggled.

"Mine. A living mortal to do with as I please. For all eternity. No need to return you or find a way to fix you. Just service whenever I please."

I quailed.

"Oh," he murmured. "Did you think that because you're mortal you can die here?"

He shook his head.

"There is no real death when you're not of my world. You were on borrowed time before and so I could have broken you far too easily. Now that you're mine and you can't die here, I can use you over and over in ever so many delicious ways and you will return to pristine state when I'm done, ready to be serviced again."

The feeling of panic came back full force. What had I done? I got a flash of a torture chamber with myriad horrendous equipment and even more deviant sexual escapades. I imagined myself brought to the limits of death, pained and agonized but without being able to feel the release of expiration.

I realized exactly how horrific hell was now.

The ethereals relived moments of torture and torment for his pleasure, but I imagined that it was mental and psychic torture, not the feeling of physical pain. I began to understand why he was so excited to have a living mortal in his realm.

I backed away. Foolishly, I had bartered away my one opportunity to escape. Kassie could have stayed here for an eternity and felt nothing. Safely behind the partition, untouched because she was special.

What made me special was exactly the opposite. He would want to use me. For my every step backward, he took one toward me. He advanced on me purposefully. The equipment behind him loomed out of the shadows.

My jeans tore from my legs with a ripping sound and fell away, leaving me naked. I clutched at my breasts and hips, vainly trying to cover myself. I expected to feel cold, but my skin flushed with heat.

The touch of leather whispered against my skin and I looked down to see it appearing from nowhere, like the man from the trenches.

"We'll start with something simple," he said. "Full restraints, I think. Face mask."

He laid a fleshy finger against his mouth when I couldn't stop a whimper. "There is no safe word."

The bastard was loving my fear. Getting off on it. And I could do was stand there, chest heaving, throat thick with a scream that wouldn't erupt.

It was no surprise my legs gave way. I collapsed in a heap and something in my knee shrieked out in pain as I landed awkwardly.

"You can't run," he said.

I stared at the mermaid's tail that used to be my legs but were now a sheath of wide leather encasing both limbs. No wonder my knee hurt; the leather was so tight they couldn't move of their own in any natural manner.

I couldn't run; he was right. If I managed to stand again, walking would be no more than a penguin's waddle.

And the leather kept coming.

All I could do was crawl along by my forearms as the garments wove themselves around me. My throat felt tight and I realized a studded collar was clutching itself around my throat.

But his toys were everywhere. Each of his collectors' items lay strewn about the floor from the crash. My hands landed on a voodoo doll and I heaved it in his direction.

He let it smack him flat in the shins.

Aim higher next time, the look on his face said. I sobbed and bit down on it as it hiccupped out of me. I couldn't lose it. Not yet. Not while I could still fight.

My hand fell on a book. It felt rough and leathery. The witch's grimoire. I plucked it from the floor with two hands and flung myself into a yoga sit up.

I used the thrust to heave it toward him. Because he was already crouching down to grab me, it slapped him in the face.

"That's right," he said. "Fight. I should like that."

He extended his arm sideways and from thin air pulled a cat o' nine tails whip.

At the same moment, I heard the teeth of a zipper biting together and I realized that the hood was pulling itself around the back of my head, stretching toward my face. Soon I wouldn't be able to see. Breathe.

Sweet Jesus. He'd waited to pull the hood up last. He wanted me to see that whip. He wanted me to give into my fear.

I groaned deep in my throat, terrified.

Not going to happen, I told myself. It just wasn't going to happen. I had to find a solution.

My ears felt stuffed with cotton, magnifying the rapid sound of my heartbeat. Soon I'd be encased in leather and vinyl and I'd have no way to see what was coming at me.

I scrabbled about, searching for something else to throw at him before the mask could cover my face. My hand wrapped around something cold. Something long and hefty.

I heaved myself over onto my back, holding it in front of me. The ascent of the material stopped.

I blinked in surprise. He was squatting in front of me, the whip over his shoulder. My stomach strained to hold me upright, the spear of mortal pain and death balanced precariously against the soles of my feet and shoulder.

It was heavy. Far too heavy for one person to wield let alone throw.

"Drop it," he said. "Drop it."

I wanted to drop it, that was for sure. It burned my hands and feet, and it sizzled as though it wanted to taste the air.

I had no idea how hard a throw I would need to make. I just prayed.

My fingers searched for a trigger in the vain hope I wouldn't have to chuck it. It started to slip out of balance. My whole body trembled with effort. Sweat dripped down my temple and leaked beneath a fold of hot leather.

I wrapped my toes around the other end to balance it.

"Don't come any further," I said. "I swear I'll use it."

He laughed. "You think you're Chu Chulain," he said. "He was a warrior. You are a plaything."

Then he lunged at me.

CHAPTER 31

My foot spasmed in reflex. My palms felt as though they'd been set alight as the spear chafed them in its haste to fly from my grip.

For a second, I thought I was done for.

But then he froze and made a sound of surprise. He stared ahead in pensive thought and then leveled that gaze to mine. Something sparked in his gaze that reminded me of a campfire flaring up in the dark of a starless sky.

My body sagged in release and I fell to my side, relieved of the heavy weight. My muscles quivered with exhaustion.

The spear had sought a home in his thigh. It jutted out so close to me I knew I could touch it with my toe if I'd had the strength to lift my leg. Then a sharp whistle cut through the air. I watched horrified as it flung out a dozen more barbs and they caught in his skin.

He didn't yell out in pain. Instead, he stopped short, looking down at himself in wonder. His gaze tracked the length of the spear to the dozen offshoots of barbs that were stuck in his neck, his arms, torso and legs. Three of them caught directly in his belly, and I watched as steam emitted from the wounds.

I scooched backwards, worming my way toward the wall as fast as I could.

In a mortal man, I would've expected his knees to buckle, but Lucifer took several more steps toward me, his movements jerky as though he was trying to run through thick liquid.

Black and viscous fluid ran from the wounds and caught fire as they met the air. He didn't try to pat them out, rather he gripped the main shaft of the spear with both of his hands and yanked on it.

His skin stretched out obscenely as he yanked on the hilt. He grunted as though he thought sheer power could dislodge the barbs from his flesh. When he eased up on the pressure, it appeared as though each shaft dug further in. The grimace on his face told me I was right.

He sucked in a deep breath and I had the feeling he was hurt.

Hurt and angry.

He was three feet away from me and no more when he dropped his head back and roared toward the ceiling. The shaft vibrated in the air with each movement. Watching it was like staring at a hypnotist's watch.

"You might think you've won," he growled as he swung that black gaze to mine. "But you still have no way out. And I have nothing but time."

He was right and we both knew it. My panic had made me stupid. Now instead of a lecherous psychopath, I had an angry one. I clutched my stomach, feeling as though I would vomit.

"Let me help you with it," I said, trying to find a way to make this awfulness better. "Let me remove it."

His head snapped up. "And what?" he said. "I'll send you home?"

He laughed under his breath. "Stupid human. You still haven't figured out that you're stuck here. Mine for all eternity. The Lilith stone is gone with the Morrigan. There is no way out for you."

He pulled at the shaft again. "It's nothing but an intermission, this."

He trod toward me. The shaft of the spear quaked with each step, echoing the quivering of my stomach. I wished I could vomit up the fear or drown out the sound of my heart pounding in my ears. The hangover of terror was deafening.

"Let me help," I squeaked out. I crawled on my forearms toward a knife that had spilled in the crash.

He held my eye with his. "I don't need help from a mortal. Watch and learn what sort of god you serve."

He grabbed the Ripper's knife from a peg, one of the only artifacts to still remain in its place. With it he sliced through his skin. He had to go deep, and it looked painful.

I could see glistening organs and dark, viscous fluid gaping out around the entry wounds. He sent fingers rummaging into the injuries one by one to extricate the barbs from his tangles of flesh.

Loud sucking sounds accompanied the liberation of each one and I did vomit, finally, leaning over onto my side and letting go a stream of bile that wrenched my gallbladder. I sagged against the glassy tiles when it was over, looking at my reflection and feeling as though I was a wet and wrung out rag. I'd been kidding myself to think I might get out of this.

There was no escape.

Maybe all I could do now was lie motionless, a limp doll with her stuffing coming out of the seams. I laid my forehead against the glass floor, wishing it wasn't so hot. I was drenched in sweat and thirsty. So thirsty.

My belly quivered against the glass floor. I could feel it touching down like a moth and then lifting off again. I'd be stuck here for eternity, dressed in a vinyl mermaid's tail and metal studded bra, servicing the Lord of darkness in painful and torturous ways until he finally tired of me.

If he ever tired of me.

Maybe it was my fate, after all. To belong to someone else. To live at their whim. Do their bidding and lose myself, my soul in the process.

Thankfully, my arms were still free, and I lay them out at my sides, palms down like a supplicant in front of the cross. I sobbed as I did so, letting the hot tears drop one by one onto the floor and pool beneath my mouth.

Surrender, I told myself. That's what I was meant for. That's all I was good for. Painful, eventual surrender.

Had I really ever had a choice?

I felt almost serene.

A grunt sounded from behind me as the spear struck the floor with a clatter. It skittered across the tiles to rest within my view but out of my reach. Of course, out of reach.

I squeezed my eyes closed in defeat. I'd done my best.

"I presume you'd like to try that again," he said from behind me. "But be warned; this is just foreplay for me. And the delay does nothing but whet my appetite."

I craned my neck to peer over my shoulder. The Lord of Hell loomed over me, his chest glistening with blood and sweat and his face swathed in lust.

He kicked the spear toward me with a wry grin.

It sailed across the tiles and butted into the heel of my hand.

He thought me weak.

Powerless.

He didn't think I would use it. He was taunting me. Arrogant and entitled, he wanted me to try and fail again. Goading me into taking the chance that would lead to failure yet again, so I could hope and lose and then loathe myself for being a failure.

I felt my lips curl in rage and hatred. He'd almost tricked me. But like most men, he underestimated me. The moment I had run from Scottie, was the moment I had truly been reborn. I wasn't the same person. I would never be the same person. No man would control me. Not Scottie, not Lucifer himself.

If he wanted me, he'd have to take me kicking and screaming and biting.

I rolled over, grappling for the spear even as it tried to skitter out of my reach.

Lucifer lumbered toward me from behind. I could hear his bare feet pounding on the tiles.

But I had it. It was in my hand. All I had to do was heft it. I had to find the strength. If I had to dig deep a thousand times in this eternity, I had to find the strength.

I might have found it; I'd never know.

Because even as he reached down to pluck me from the floor, the entire chamber shook.

Lucifer staggered on his feet, falling backwards and upending into a pile of the relics he loved so much.

He swung his gaze to mine as though it was something I was making happen.

I eyed the spear, thinking for a moment that perhaps it had some special powers neither of us was aware of. I almost expected it to be lit from within or buzzing or a different color.

It lay inert in my palm and an unearthly screech cut through the air.

It wasn't the spear doing any of it.

Something else, maybe something more fearsome than Lucifer himself had entered his realm and by the look on his face, he was enraged.

I gripped the hilt of the spear tightly. Whatever was coming, I'd fight to the last.

"Morrigan," Lucifer hissed and struggled to get to his feet. He kicked aside the items he'd been so proud of before and strode to face her.

She took an elegant and languid step toward him. Over her arm was slung a tattered green silk swath of material that looked like it was covered in blood. My dress.

The Morrigan, I realized. Whole and hale with all three parts of her godliness merged together again. Somewhere in the depths of her expression, I recognized Kassie the teenager. But it was a remote resemblance at best. This Morrigan was regal and statuesque. Even her deportment gave the impression of magnificence. She was calm and collected even in the face of Lucifer's glower.

She had nothing to fear from him.

Next to her stood a quaking brunette. Slim and average sized, she clung to the Morrigan like a child about to get a spanking.

"I have something that belongs to you," the Morrigan said. "Something I think you will be happy to have returned."

She gave a gentle shove to the woman clutching at her. Ismé, I realized. The woman who had betrayed Kassie and sold her to Gio so that she could regain her freedom.

"A vampire," he said with disgust. "I have thousands of them."

"Not just a vampire," the Morrigan said. "Look again."

He canted his head as he slid his black gaze over Ismé's quaking form. "One with a soul," he said with a gasp of pleasure.

"Yes. You gave her release in exchange for information on me. You know how that turned out," the Morrrigan said. "But what you don't know is that when she returned to the ninth world, that soul of hers jumped into a vulnerable female. And she let a vampire turn her."

She looked at Ismé with disgust and revulsion. "She's a sociopath. A perfect fit for you."

He narrowed his gaze as he squinted at the Morrigan. "So I'm not bound by the Lilith stone?" he asked. "She has no time limit?"

The Morrigan inclined her head in a nod. "She's as good as a living mortal but without the constraints of time here in your dead world."

"What do you want in return?"

She swung her gaze to me. "My blood is joined to this human," she said. "You have no rights to her."

That made him furious. "That's not true. She is mine. I won her. You abandoned her."

She canted her head at him. "I didn't abandon her. I needed to return to myself, to gather myself together. Now I'm here and I want to bring her back where she belongs."

"You can't have her."

She shook her head. "Unfortunately, you have no say. Take the gift I've offered and be glad of it."

She reached her hand out to me and because I was loathe to let go of the spear, I gripped her fingers with my free one.

The next thing I knew I felt as though every particle of my body was squeezing down into one small compressed molecule. Some part of me prayed that I wouldn't end up in a lake somewhere in the human world, drowning the way I had when I'd arrived at Lucifer's tub.

But the time passed quickly this time and instead of feeling as though I was between worlds, I felt like I stepped over a threshold.

It took a second to realize I was back in my apartment, standing next to the sofa and clutching Kassie's hand so tightly that my knuckles were white. When she peeled her hand away from mine my fingers stayed curled in a fist.

Except it wasn't Kassie of course. It was the Morrigan. Her hair swept the bottom of her back and now that we were in a world with regular lighting, I could see the last inch of her hair was the deepest shade of red, as though it had been trailing in pools of blood.

Of course, it probably had. I remembered her washing my dress, the puddle she had knelt over in Fayed's alley. The adrenaline soaking my tissues left all at once and my vision dimmed.

I was going to faint. I reached out for something to catch me and realized I was still holding onto the spear.

I dropped it as I weaved on my feet. It made a dull thudding sound where it struck the mat. I eyed it with an odd sense of detachment. It was still covered in tissues and black blood and it stank of smoke and vomit.

My stomach heaved, and I buckled over. For some reason, I felt wobbly, unable to move my legs. They felt glued together.

Delicate hands caught me and smoothed my back as I struggled to keep my stomach lining from exiting through my nose.

Shivers ran the length of my spine as I shuddered and twisted to look up at her. She smiled and ran her hand down my hair.

"My warrior," she said. "I knew you could do it."

Somewhere in my befuddled mind I registered her words. I knew you could do it. As though she had set me up. As though she had known all along that I would end up going to hell to reclaim her. As though she were entitled to such a thing.

No word of concern for my welfare, of gratitude for what I'd endured on her behalf. I was fodder for their playground. A relic like the one Lucifer collected. I'd cared about her. Worried for her safety.

It didn't matter that she had retrieved me from hell, saved me from God knows what. It was bad enough that she was the reason I was there in the first place.

I pushed away from her, sick of being used by the supernatural creatures who felt entitled to exploit my vulnerability.

No better than Scottie. Any of them.

I found the couch with my palm and ran a trembling hand along it to be sure it was really there. That it was soft and solid and would hold me when I fell onto it because I most definitely was going to fall. My knees wouldn't bend right. I tried to take a step and I did fall. Onto the floor beside the sofa.

My hand met resistance, and then a shadow I'd not seen shifted.

The sidhe warlord. Sitting there, watching it all and staying silent.

CHAPTER 32

"Fuck," I said before I could stop it.

I yanked my hand back and pinwheeled away from both of them. Of course, I fell on my backside because I still couldn't move my feet independently.

She stood like the goddess she was, regal and straight. He lounged on the sofa with one leg over the other, crossed at the knee. His foot was bobbing up and down as he fidgeted.

"Nice outfit," he said. "Going to a party?"

I looked down at myself. The vinyl sheathing that stretched across my legs sent my mind streaking back to Lucifer's boudoir.

I sobbed in spite of myself. I was still wearing that awful garb. I tried to tear it off, digging my nails in as I searched for laces or zippers.

It was the Morrigan who stopped me. She slipped a thin nail into a crease and slid her finger downward. The vinyl split without a sound.

The spear lay at the Morrigan's feet. She tracked my gaze as it landed on the hilt. She bent to retrieve the spear from the floor and handed it to Colin, hilt end first.

"Perhaps this will repay the debt," she said.

He looked at it for a long time before he stood and wrapped his fingers around the grip. They stared at each other for long moments.

"Eons of immortality I didn't want," he said, sounding less than grateful. "A death I didn't deserve at an age far too young, a week in hell defending my honour."

He pulled the spear from her grip and wiped it on his arm. The blood that had coated the tip and now was smeared over his perfectly tailored shirt turned blue. "Small things, really, in the grand scheme of things."

He stared at her. "This will grant my forgiveness," he said. "But the debt remains." His jaw set into a hard line that made him look more the warrior he must have been in his days as a mortal.

Even I could see that she looked crestfallen at his response. I felt cheated that this was the way it was going to end up.

"You've got to be kidding," I said. "Do you know what I went through down there?"

He swung that prismic gaze to mine. "Technically, down is not where you went, but yes. I have a very good idea."

I shifted uncomfortably under that gaze. He had suffered as I had suffered. Perhaps more so. I should understand that gratitude for being alive didn't necessarily wipe out the sense of injustice in the first place.

The Morrigan clenched her fists at her side.

"I will endure another century as a broken thing if it will satisfy you," she said. I heard in her voice the longing of a lover, one spurned but not yet ready to concede defeat.

I was uncomfortable with the look on the Fae's face. He wasn't willing to give in. He felt as though a debt was still owed even after all she had gone through, even after what he'd put me through to retrieve her from Lucifer.

I wasn't angry that he'd elected to send me instead of himself. I understood that. Having been there, having seen what Lucifer would do to those things he considered his property, I couldn't blame him.

I could be angry about having to go through it, and I could be sad that all of those creatures below, those ethereals as he'd called them, would be acting as his playthings for the next eternity, but I could not blame Chu Chulain for wanting to avoid the terror of that place.

So, he had wanted someone to risk it for this woman he didn't love. This powerful goddess who was willing to give him everything.

There had to be a reason.

What did he want if he didn't want her to repay her debt and find absolution from him.

And then it occurred to me. He hadn't sent me to rescue Kassie at all. He just wanted his weapon back. I thought of the creatures in the Shadow Bazaar and how they tried to help Kassie when the fae assassin held her.

I thought of Maddox's explanation that they wanted to curry favor. Someday she might feel inclined to intervene for them.

He knew that too.

He wanted the spear. He knew the Morrigan would want to repay her debt if he found a way to extract her from Lucifer. He knew he'd left it behind in Hell and that Gio had bartered Kassie's flesh for his soul.

"It was a perfect storm," I said. "A mortal who owed you. A mortal who cared about a vulnerable teenager not knowing she was the physical aspect of a god who betrayed you. That's why you gave me that talisman; you knew Lucifer would be unable to resist living flesh."

"The Lilith Stone should have got you out too," he said. "I'm not a monster. It had enough power to transport you both."

His eyes glowed blue, as though he dared me to believe he was lying.

The truth was, I believed he was sincere. But it was hard to see sentiment in the blood coating his sleeve, at the way he held onto the spear as though he planned to put it to use with zeal. A warrior. To his core, although he was sidhe now and might never need it to do harm.

"But I couldn't use the talisman because Lucifer held me back," I said, and I remembered the feeling of wanting one of us safe after all that. "One of us had the chance to use it. I gave it to her."

I studied the Morrigan and the stiff way she held herself, no doubt remembering the stasis, the feeling of being frozen, at the mercy of a dark angel and the whims of a mortal.

I wondered if she recalled that one moment when one of us had the chance to escape and I'd sacrificed my own because I wanted my pain to be worth something.

Her eyes lingered too long on Chu Chulain's jawline, a little too softly for her to be upset at the way things turned out.

She was a fate, *the* fate, according to Lucifer. Able to intervene, knowing the outcome even before it was set in motion.

"Oh my God," I said with a gasp and she turned that black gaze to mine. "You knew all along, didn't you?"

A slow smile threaded onto her face. "Fate is a curious thing," she said.

She had known. Since the day she used a blood connection to get me into the Shadow Bazaar, she had known. She might even have known before then.

The truth of it was she wanted that connection because she knew it would allow me into Hell to seize her, to bring her back, to allow herself to repay a debt of shame she owed this warrior.

Maybe she had been the one to put it all into motion.

Looking at her, I had no doubt she had even shown me a teenaged aspect of herself because she knew I'd connect with it in a visceral way, the lost Isabella who still had a hope of being undamaged before she'd chosen a man who would damage her in ways she would never be free of.

The parallels to my time in Hell were too close for comfort.

I looked at her again, this creature I'd thought was a runaway teenager. This runaway god. She'd played a long game, maybe one she'd set in motion the day she'd tricked Chu Chulain into eating dog flesh, sealing his fate to Lucifer's hounds, and sealing her own.

She smiled wanly at me. "Thank you," she said. "For being willing to save me for love instead of favor."

She pressed a velveteen pouch into my hand and closed my fingers around it.

"Keep it always in this enchanted bag," she said, and just like that, she was gone. She didn't fade. She didn't blur out. Just disappeared as though she was never there.

I turned to the sidhe, feeling less than charitable. I was exhausted and spent and sore everywhere and yet this was still far from over.

"Well, I did what you wanted," I said baldly. All emotion had left me except for the flavor of rage that was encroaching up my throat. "My debt to you is done."

He inclined his head. "Of course."

I eyed him.

"What will it cost to keep the portal live?" I said.

He grinned. "You catch on quickly."

"I wouldn't say quickly," I said, thinking of the events of the last few days. But it was the slant of his head, the way he wouldn't look me in the eye that was the most telling.

He wasn't about to guarantee not to strong-arm me again. He wanted me to owe him indefinitely and that portal shift between worlds meant he had a perpetual debt.

He wouldn't absolve the Morrigan; he wouldn't absolve me either.

"I've paid," I said. "Now take it off. I don't want your magics anymore."

He lifted a silvery brow and hefted the spear in his hand, flexing his fingers around it. "Are you sure?" he said. "You do still have enemies."

I heaved a long sigh. "I can't rely on magic anymore. It comes with too big a price tag."

This time when he smiled, there was no malice in it.

He looked relieved.

"It took me a century to learn that," he said. "In gratitude, I'll let you leave through the door before I destroy the portal. Give you a head start on the man who's waiting for you."

I nodded with a tight throat. Scottie. Of course he would still be there. He was a bulldog.

I took a step toward the door and realized I was barefoot. And that the vinyl sheathing and studded collar might be hard to blend in my neighborhood.

Chu Chulain must have noticed because he reached down toward the sofa arm and lifted the green dress from its arm.

"She left this," he said and proffered it.

I took it without a word of thanks.

"Goodbye, Ms. Hush," he said softly. "You might not think so, but you are a warrior."

With that, he turned heel and left me alone to strip out of the leather and vinyl and pull on the dress. It smelled of sunshine and clothes dried on an old-fashioned line.

I was barefoot and clad in a gown far too elegant for what I was about to do, but at least it didn't stink of blood and smoke.

I shook my hands out at my sides and with a deep breath headed for the front door.

I still had to face Scottie.

CHAPTER 33

IT WAS A GREAT leap of faith to step out onto the Brownstone stoop and know that behind me, within the confines of my apartment, the portal that had kept me safe over the last few weeks was gone and would never return.

I felt something warm and fuzzy curling around my calf. Soft and padded feet touched down on my instep. I looked down to see my cat twining around my ankles. Next to her sat a hefty duffel bag. I didn't need to unzip it or look inside to know that it was filled with clothes and equipment.

Somehow Colin had given me one last gift. The ability to walk away from Scottie with everything I needed.

But it was the sight of my cat and the sound of her purring as she touched my skin that decided me. She was a scrapper. She had always been one since the time I'd met her as a kitten. She was small and skinny and as full of piss and vinegar as a full-grown alley tomcat.

If I walked away now, Scottie would always follow me. If I went back inside and faced him, he would undoubtedly drag me back with him to the safety of his gang.

And then as promised, he would show each and every one of them who was boss. He would reclaim his dignity and I would lose mine.

And he would think that an even bargain.

I bent to scoop the cat from the step and rubbed my face in her fragrant fur. She smelled of toffee and lemons. She batted at my cheek with her paw but kept her claws pulled in.

I'd suffered a moment of defeat in Hell. I'd forgotten I was strong. A warrior, the Morrigan said. So had the sidhe. Maybe I was and maybe I wasn't, but one thing was for sure: I couldn't live with the constant dread of Scottie's specter over me, waiting to touch down at any time like a bomb.

I needed a clean slate.

I heaved a sigh and spun on my bare foot to push open the door. I tossed the cat into the foyer and dropped the duffel bag down at the bottom of the stairs.

At first, I thought perhaps the apartment was empty. I heard no sounds coming from within. But as I turned to look inside, I noticed that the entire apartment had been ransacked. I usually left socks and shoes and clothes and dishes lying around, but this was nothing like that.

Every single drawer was upended onto the tiles and then dropped atop the contents. The cupboard doors were flung open and dishes pulled out onto the floor. I winced as I remembered my bare feet and knew that glass shards were no doubt sprayed everywhere.

The cat streaked for my bedroom, leaving me alone to face the man sitting on the sofa the way the Fae had done. His arms were stretched across the back and he settled into the cushions on the only place in the entire apartment that was free of debris.

My hands curled into fists against my dress and knotted up the material. I could do this.

He was just a man after all.

"Where the hell have you been?" he said.

If only he knew how close to reality that question was.

I bent quietly to scoop things from the floor, gathering shoes and socks and underwear the way I was gathering my thoughts.

How far did I want to go? How badly did I want to be removed from the thing that was Scottie?

I had the talisman. I knew exactly what it did. I could pull it from its pouch and pass it to him as though I'd found the greatest treasure. He would take it, no doubt. Entitled to whatever was mine.

But was he really that bad after all? Did he really deserve to go to hell?

I had been lucky to get out. I'd had Kassie. Scottie would have no one. And he would be everything Lucifer would want. A living mortal with a penchant for violence and anger. Scottie himself was a warrior. Built for it, he would give Lucifer a hell of a run for his money.

Scottie had no idea of the other world. I had no doubt he would waste precious time trying to figure out where he was, and even if he began to believe the evidence of his senses, he wouldn't be prepared to spar verbally with the devil.

I had no doubt that Lucifer would run out his time the way he'd almost run out mine. And then the talisman would go back to wherever it came from and Scottie would be left there for an eternity.

I didn't care how bad he was. No one deserved that.

"Well?" he said and this time there was no patience in his voice.

I could feel him standing up from behind me. I knew that if I turned he would be clenching his fists, his fair face flushed with anger. His fury was echoed in the way every piece of my belongings was broken or strewn carelessly about the room.

No mention of how I must have just simply disappeared in front of his eyes.

I wondered if the talisman had some power to wipe a memory clean, or to show someone exiting the building as though they had just spun on heel and left. How had he explained my disappearance to himself?

I turned around slowly, all the better to make sure he didn't think I had a weapon of any sort. I held my hands up in front of me, supplicating and surrendering. Just the way he would like it.

If there had been room on the floor, I would have fallen to my knees. Kiss his feet the way any arrogant god would like.

"Where do you think I went?" I said. I took a tentative step forward.

"I'll be damned how you got out of my grasp and into the bathroom," he said. "But I have to give it to you, Sis, you're good at squeezing in and out of tight places."

I looked over toward my bathroom door which was ajar. The curtains fluttered in the breeze inward. He must've thought I'd got away from him and crawled out the window.

"I needed some time to think," I stammered out.

His face looked like a boiled ham. "Think?" He said. "You left me here for hours. What is there to think about? You're coming with me."

"I had a lot to think about," I said. "Us, for example."

"You're as slippery as an eel," he complained, ignoring my comment. "But I'll be fixing that when we get back."

"That's what I was thinking about," I said. "I have a proposition. One I think that will be very useful to you, to us."

"What kind of proposition?"

"One year," I said, holding up my index finger.

I noticed his glance went to the black velvet pouch clutched in my palm, held immobile there by the other three fingers.

He wanted to ask me what it was. I needed to lay the groundwork before he asked.

So I hurried on, holding up the pouch so he could get clear view of it. "This," I said. "This is the key."

"What is it?" He wasn't softening but he was interested. His greed always won out.

"A weapon," I said, letting my experience with the fae guide me. Tell him some. Leave out the details. "One the right people will pay dearly for."

He squinted at me, suspicious. "What kind of weapon would fit in a little bag?"

"A powerful one," I said. "But my contacts are still working on its trigger and how to harness it properly. It's all in research. I promise you. I haven't just been sitting on my hands out here."

I took another step closer, letting it dangle from my fingers. "I can't leave now. I'm too close. Made too many contacts."

"You think I'm stupid," he said.

"No," I hurried. "Never. You just don't have all the contacts. Alvin found me here with one of them. He was the one who hurt Alvin. Not me."

I held out the pouch. "For this. That's how valuable this is."

He didn't believe me, but he wanted to. Thought of a valuable item that might be within his reach was just too good to let go without consideration. He didn't want to make a mistake he'd regret.

"You need a year to figure it out?" he said.

"Yes. It's deadly secretive stuff I've got myself into and I need time to get my affairs in order, to finish up the last of the negotiations. These people won't deal easily or with someone they've not met. What do you think I've been doing here for three years?"

He inhaled deeply, and I thought perhaps he was considering it. Then he shook his head no.

"No," he said. "You're mine."

"I'm not disputing that," I said. "But think about it. You can tell your people you have me stationed here. I'll send you tributes to prove it."

His jaw seesawed back and forth. He might not have believed me if I hadn't thrown in the bit about Alvin. He knew I couldn't do that sort of damage to the thug, and he knew I'd had help.

He would want to believe the person who did it was greedy rather than laying me down in bed each night. His ego didn't want to believe it.

I could see him shifting his thinking. He stared at the pouch with a greedy eye.

"I want possession," he said.

I shook my head slowly, as though to dissuade him. "I don't know..." I said, letting it trail off.

"Give it to me, Sis. If we're going to do this, I need to have possession."

I let go a long-suffering sigh and held it out into the space between us.

"Don't open it," I said. "I mean it. The results could be disastrous, and we have no idea how bad yet."

He eyed it with a gleam in his eye.

"One year," he said, lifting the pouch from my fingers and pocketing it. "You report once a month, not quarterly, through Skype so everyone can see you."

I nodded, not wanting to look too eager.

"And you pay me 75% of what you bring in."

I opened my mouth to protest as he expected. He glared at me, expecting me to wince under his gaze. "Seventy five percent."

"Alright," I said. I didn't want to heave a relieved sigh. It was too soon. I waited until he approached the door and pulled it open before I collapsed onto the sofa.

I'd taken my life back in hand. I'd left Scottie's fate to his own choices. If he opened the pouch, he'd bring whatever hell had onto himself.

If he trusted me, at least I'd be living on my own terms.

And anything could happen in a year.

I lay back on the sofa with my arm flung over the arm, thinking about dealing with the devil and wondering how I was going to earn enough in the next month to persuade Scottie, if he lived that long, that I was doing exactly what he wanted.

And as fate would have it, I looked up to see Maddox peering down at me.

"Hello, Kitten," he said. "How was your nap?"

"Was I sleeping?" I said, not concerned that he'd walked into my apartment in the least. In fact, I rather enjoyed waking up to that face.

He smiled down at me. "Snoring," he said.

I sat up. Stretched.

"What time is it?" I said.

He pushed beside me on the sofa, shooting me a heart-stopping grin.

"Time to offer you a proposition."

<<<<*Finitio*>>>>

Continue the series with Stone Goddess and fall back into a world of intrigue and magic.

GET EXCLUSIVE BONUS Scenes from the series

ACKNOWLEDGMENTS

Several loyal readers have special places in my writer's heart. Some of them, like Caroline Jenkins and Denise Sherman always take the time to find my little oopsies and sometimes my big ones. An author needs readers like that.

Then there's readers like Crystal Crystal Amason, who isn't just a reader, she's a sponsor, and you don't get more loyal than that. She is the first reader to make me feel like my tales were worth reading. Thank you, Crystal. I hope I can continue to write stories you enjoy.

To my other patrons who prefer to remain anonymous, I thank you. You know who you are.

I really appreciate you all.

-thea-